I study my legs. Mrs. Friendly has no idea what it's like for me. No one does. Everyone keeps spouting inspirational phrases like they'll change my life, but the words feel as empty as the printed poems on all the sympathy cards we got after Dad died. Words won't turn back time. Words can't fix my legs.

Also by Antony John

The Other, Better Me

ANTONY JOHN

HARPER

An Imprint of HarperCollins Publishers

Library of Congress Control Number: 2018938255

ISBN 978-0-06-283563-5

Typography by Aurora Parlagreco

19 20 21 22 23   PC/BRR   10 9 8 7 6 5 4 3 2 1

❖

First paperback edition, 2019

To Brenda Kukay, Kirsten Shaw, and school librarians across Missouri—you're rock stars in my book

DOUBLE-WIDE

The new kid is large. Taller than our homeroom teacher, Ms. Guthrie, and as wide as her desk. Okay, maybe not *that* wide, but he's prime bully material.

Believe me, I ought to know.

"You must be Ruben," Ms. Guthrie says.

"That is correct," he says. Then, before she can ask us to give him a warm Wellspring Middle School welcome, Ruben continues. "My full name is Ruben Spencer Hardesty. My family just moved here to St. Louis from Albuquerque. My hobbies are doing puzzle books and hacking the parental controls on my father's laptop. I also like astronomy but not astrology, because they're not the same thing at all, even though people get them mixed up. My parents say that sometimes I provide too much information."

"No kidding," mutters Logan Montgomery, who until today was the biggest kid in seventh grade.

"However," continues Ruben, "I've been told that explaining my interests is the fastest way to find friends who are like me."

"Good luck with that," snorts Logan.

Usually Ms. Guthrie would give Logan a warning. Not this time, though. Right now, our teacher has this crazy frozen smile, like she's auditioning to be the fifth face on Mount Rushmore. "Wow," she says.

She's not the only one wearing a weird expression. Pretty much everyone looks confused by the new arrival with the tentlike, green polo shirt and heavily gelled hair.

Not me, though. I'm starting to like Ruben. Because the way I see it, there are only two possible explanations for his little introduction.

(1) He's crazy.

(2) He's a total genius who knows that the new kid can get away with saying *anything*, so he's putting on a show.

Either way, he's the center of attention right now, and that's fine by me. At least it is until Ms. Guthrie points to the empty seat beside me and tells him, "You can sit over there."

Big kid with big mouth gets stuck next to snarky kid in wheelchair. Misfits unite!

He trundles over to me and holds out his hand. "I'm Ruben."

"Noah Savino," I say. I really don't want to shake hands, not with everyone in class watching us, but Ruben's just standing there like a waxwork figure. So I do it anyway.

A snicker ripples through the room.

"Ruben Spencer Hardesty, huh?" I say, trying to keep the focus on him. "That's an impressive name."

His eyes seem to be fixed on my shoes. (Converse All Stars. Very retro.) "At my old school, everyone called me Double-Wide," he says.

I figure I misheard him. "Double-Wide?"

"Because I'm so big."

I can't believe he just admitted that. *Out loud.* Next, he'll be telling me he doesn't believe in personal hygiene and that he likes to sacrifice bunny rabbits every full moon. Behind him, Ms. Guthrie glares at everyone—a warning to keep their mouths shut.

"You're not *so* big," I say, trying to help him out.

"Yes, I am. I'm taller than 99.3 percent of my peers, and I

have a body mass index of 26.5, which means I'm obese." He nods to himself. "So you can see, my nickname is backed up by objective data."

"Uh . . ."

"Please take a seat, Ruben," says Ms. Guthrie, looking just as freaked out as I feel. "There's space at Noah's desk."

Actually, there are two spaces, and Double-Wide fills both of them. His nickname is quite accurate, it turns out.

He places his book bag gently in his lap and turns to me. "You're in a wheelchair."

I roll my eyes. "And you're very observant. Got any other special skills?"

"Well, I know pi to two hundred decimal places."

"That must come in handy."

He thinks about this. "Not very often."

"Shocker."

He nods. "So why are you in a wheelchair?"

"Because I'm too lazy to walk."

"Will they let me have a wheelchair too?"

"Probably not."

"Hmm." He opens his bag and pulls out a Batman pencil case. I can't remember the last time I saw a Batman pencil case. I wonder if he's got a Disney lunch box in there too.

4

He catches me gawking. "Cool, isn't it?"

"Uh . . ."

Ms. Guthrie clears her throat. Double-Wide leans closer to me. "Looks like class is starting," he stage whispers. "I guess we should concentrate now, Noah."

I could point out that this is homeroom, not class, but I don't think it'd make any difference. Double-Wide seems to exist in his own world.

One thing's for certain, though. I was wrong when I said he was prime bully material. If anything, he's prime bully*ing* material.

Again, I ought to know.

A FORCEFUL PAIR

After homeroom, Double-Wide follows me to math. And I do mean *follow*. If we were side by side, we'd take up the entire hallway.

He has a hard time keeping up. I could probably leave him behind, but I don't want to be a jerk, so I ease off the throttle. And by *throttle*, I mean my arms. My upper body works well, but the lower half . . . Well, let's just say that my wheelchair and I are pretty much inseparable.

It could be worse, I guess. My chair is a good one: super lightweight aluminum, with adjustable-tension upholstery and high-pressure tires. If it were a car, it'd be a Corvette.

But if it were a Corvette, it'd have an engine and then people would hear me coming and move out of my way—instead of what *actually* happens, which is that no one hears me coming at all. Even when I accidentally ram people from behind, I can't seem to make them budge. Believe me, I've tried.

It wasn't always like this. On the first day of middle school last year, I walked into the building on my own two legs. I was even the starting catcher for one of the best Little League teams in St. Louis.

Then came the car accident. That was in April. By the time I woke up in St. Louis Children's Hospital, my legs and brain weren't on talking terms anymore and my internal organs had been rearranged. I spent the next two months as a guest at the twelfth-floor neurorehab center, along with six other kids whose luck was just as good as mine. It was almost July when I finally went home. A counselor told Mom it was important for me to establish routines, but all my old routines involved two parents. That first night, I heard Mom crying in her bedroom.

See, Dad was in the car with me the day we crashed. He didn't even make it to the hospital, though. Turns out, you don't need to be a doctor to pronounce someone dead on the hard shoulder of an interstate highway.

"Can you slow down?" says Double-Wide, interrupting my thoughts.

"Sorry." I drop from a slog to a crawl. "You doing all right?"

"Great," he wheezes.

Note to self: Double-Wide is not a convincing liar.

Logan Montgomery and his baseball posse come to a stop just ahead of us. They're blocking the hallway, so I have to apply the brakes.

For reasons I still don't understand, I was a part of this group last year. (Hey, nobody's perfect.) I guess we'd spent so much time playing ball together in the summer before sixth grade, it made sense to stick together in school too. But that all changed the day of the accident.

"So, Noah," drawls Logan, "how's the weather down there?" He flashes a smug grin.

Did I mention I'm happy to be out of his posse? Yeah, that's why. And this isn't even a new joke for Logan. He tried it out on the first day of seventh grade, three weeks ago, and it wasn't funny then either.

"Bet you get a great view of everyone's butt from that seat, huh?" he continues, displaying the full range of his comic genius.

Logan (and his fast-growing facial hair) clearly has a whole bunch of insults lined up and ready to go, and everyone is tuned in, listening. But before he can let the next one fly, Double-Wide crouches beside me.

"You know what, Noah?" says Double-Wide. "He's right. You really *do* have a good view of people's butts."

Logan isn't expecting this—heck, *no one* is expecting this—and it throws him off his game. He's probably wondering if Double-Wide is making fun of him, which must feel weird because that's Logan's specialty. Personally, I think my new companion is just doing what comes naturally: sharing whatever random thought is on his mind.

"Yeah," says Logan. "I mean . . . whatever."

As Logan lumbers away, two of my former Little League teammates, Justin and Carlos, nod their heads at me. I think they're about to say something too. But when they notice the rest of the team leaving without them, they hurry off. I can't say I blame them—none of us knows what to say to each other anymore.

The hallway traffic begins to flow again. Slowly. As we navigate the crowd, several students sneak peeks at me, the kid in the Corvette wheelchair, but their eyes drift to Double-Wide too. In his own special way, he stands out just as much as me.

It's nice to share the limelight for a change, although I'm not sure that Double-Wide notices the funny looks we're getting. I'm kind of envious.

Once we reach cruising speed—about one mile per hour, by my estimate—Double-Wide asks, "Do you know Newton's second law?"

"No," I say. "I don't know Newton's second law."

"Well, it states that *force equals mass times acceleration*. Since you have the extra weight of a wheelchair and I'm the size of a tank, our combined masses are necessarily greater than anyone around us. So as long as we accelerate at the same speed as everyone else in the hallway, our force is clearly much greater."

I look around. One, we are not moving at the same speed as everyone else. Two, I don't think anyone is watching us and thinking, *Wow, what a forceful pair!*

But so what? Ever since the accident, people have been trying to convince me that my glass is half full, but Double-Wide is the first person who sounds like he really means it.

I could do with a little honesty for a change.

3

MATH PROBLEMS

Alyssa Choo perches on the edge of my desk and crosses her legs. "Hi, Ruben," she says, waving at Double Wide. "I'm Alyssa."

Double-Wide looks confused. "Do I know you?"

"We're in the same homeroom."

"Oh. It's nice to meet you." He holds out his hand and they shake, which almost never happened at Wellspring Middle School until today. "Please, call me Double-Wide."

"O-okay," she says, producing her own version of Ms. Guthrie's freaked-out smile.

Alyssa and I have known each other since first grade. We

used to ride the bus together in elementary school. No matter how early I got to the stop, Alyssa would already be waiting, her hair tied back in pigtails and her nose in a book. She still reads plenty, but she's grown up a lot too. And I'm not just talking about her height.

"Noah," she says, "are you staring at my boobs?"

I look up sharply. "What? No!"

"I think you were," says Double-Wide helpfully. "However, that's mostly because they fall precisely at your line of sight."

Alyssa's face is all twisted up, like she's getting a whiff of stink bomb. "So you're saying it's *my* fault?"

"No," I say quickly.

"More or less," says Double-Wide.

My face is burning with the power of a thousand suns.

"I guess I'll sit down, then," she says. She slides onto the chair across the aisle from me and folds her arms across her chest. "Better?"

We're level now, and I'm looking directly at her face. "Better," I say.

I mean it too.

The classroom door opens, and our math teacher, Mr. Kostas, strides in. He seems to have an extra bounce in his step as he hands out today's warm-up work sheet.

I read the title—"Comparing Data: Numbers that actually mean something!"—and realize why he's excited. He's asking us to calculate the batting average of ten St. Louis Cardinals baseball players. Mr. Kostas is a big fan of "real-world mathematics," as he likes to tell us. All the time.

"Noah," he says before he's even made it back to his desk. "Perhaps you can explain to us what a batting average is."

There are three columns on the work sheet. The first is titled "at-bats." The second says "hits." The last column, which is blank, is headed "average." I don't think anyone needs me to explain anything. Certainly not Double-Wide, who immediately begins filling in answers.

"Noah?" continues Mr. Kostas encouragingly. "Since you're something of a baseball expert, I thought . . ."

I flush red. I am definitely *not* a baseball expert. Anymore. I also don't like being called on. So I stare at the sheet, keep quiet, and wait for him to ask someone else instead.

"I'll give you a clue," he says helpfully. "You divide one number by the other number. Do you know which way around it is?"

Everyone in the class goes quiet. Mr. Kostas is a good teacher, but why can't he just let it go? It's obvious that he feels as uncomfortable as I do. He looks like a cheerleader smiling bravely when the game is out of reach.

I want to shrink into my seat, but that's hard to do in a wheelchair, even one with adjustable-tension upholstery.

Alyssa raises her hand. "Uh, Mr. Kostas?"

"Yes, Alyssa!" Mr. Kostas latches on to her voice like a drowning man grasping a life preserver.

"I was wondering," she says, eyes fixed on the work sheet. "Are Major League Baseball statistics really the best we can do in a twenty-first-century coeducational classroom?"

Mr. Kostas looks like he's trying to translate her question into English. "Do you, uh, have a problem with baseball?"

"Not with the sport, no. Actually, I like it. But I'm sure you're aware there aren't any female players in Major League Baseball."

"Well, yes. That's obvious—"

"Or female managers."

"Uh . . ."

"Or female umpires."

Mr. Kostas is turning various shades of red. "Maybe you can change that, Ms. Choo."

Two rows back, Logan belly laughs. He's always been the best pitcher and batter for my old Little League team, so he's the real expert on all things baseball. His dad even coaches the team.

"Is something funny, Logan?" demands Mr. Kostas.

"No," says Logan, pretending to be shocked. "What could be funny about Alyssa becoming a professional baseball player?"

He turns to my former teammates, inviting them to laugh too. After a moment, they nod their heads like brainless bobblehead dolls.

"I think," says Alyssa, "that it would be more *inclusive* to use different data from now on. Like, say, number of roses per vase or cups of milk to flour in different sizes of cake."

Double-Wide looks up from his work sheet. "I agree. My father buys roses, and I like cake."

"No kidding," says Logan.

Mr. Kostas gives Logan a hard stare. "Fine," he tells Alyssa. "Everyone, please hand your work sheets back. I certainly wouldn't want anyone to think that math is sexist."

Everyone gratefully passes the work sheets to the front. All except for Double-Wide.

"Hey, Double-Wide," I whisper. "You need to stop."

It's like he doesn't hear me. All the other sheets are in now, and kids are peering over to see what he's doing. Maybe he's covering the page in graffiti. Or drawing a baseball bat, or—

Suddenly, he drops his pencil and holds up the sheet. Even flutters it gently like he's impatient for Mr. Kostas to collect it. I take a good long look at it, which is how I discover that, while we were debating whether to use baseball statistics in math, he just worked out ten batting averages without using a calculator.

Mr. Kostas adds this sheet to the pile like it's no different from any other. A part of me wants to point out that Double-Wide just completed the *whole work sheet,* but I'm not sure that drawing even more attention to my new supersized friend is the best idea. So I keep quiet.

I'm not the only one who's quiet. Standing behind his desk, Mr. Kostas stares at the pile of paper drooping from his left hand the way a preschooler looks at an ice cream cone as the scoop of creamy goodness goes splat on the ground. Then he glances at me, and suddenly everything becomes clear: today's baseball-themed work sheet wasn't for everyone. It was for *me.* A gift. An attempt to cheer me up. To get me talking again. To remind me of better times.

And what did I do? Like a Cardinals fan catching an opponent's home-run ball, I threw it right back at him.

THE DYNAMO

Dynamo Duric is unstoppable.

Don't believe me? Just ask him.

When I arrive for my physical therapy appointment at the Children's Hospital clinic, he's already lying on a mat, going through his exercises. He tilts his head as I pull alongside him. "Can't stop the Dynamo," he grunts. "The Dynamo has no off switch."

Nine-year-old boys should never talk about themselves in the third person. I'd mention this to him, but Angelica, my physical therapist (or PT, as she calls herself), is waiting.

"Noah!" she says, like seeing me is the highlight of her

week. "How's that back-to-school program we developed working out for you?"

"Not so good," I say. "Teachers are still giving me homework."

"Ha! Actually, I asked them to double up on that. Don't want you getting bored."

"That's nice."

"And don't you forget it!" she says, emphasizing each word with a finger wag. "Seriously, though. How's it going?"

It's her job to ask me this, but I think she actually cares too. Trouble is, if I answer her honestly, we might end up talking about *feelings*, and I'm so not in the mood for that.

"I've got a new friend," I say, because I know it will make her happy. It also has the advantage of being true.

"That's great!" she says. "What's he like? Or *she* . . ."

"He," I say quickly. "He's, uh, different. Kind of funny."

"Good. And what about your friends from Little League?"

"Oh, you know. Logan's still mouthing off."

"Uh-huh." She waits for me to continue, but that's all I'm giving her today. She didn't even know about the team until they tried to visit me at the hospital and I turned them away. That led to our first talk about *feelings*. I've been trying to forget about that conversation ever since.

"Okay, then," she says, all business. "How are the exercises going?"

"Great," I lie.

She claps her hands together. "So, let's see them."

I plant my hands on the wheelchair arms and push. Without the use of my legs, sliding onto the padded exercise mat used to seem impossible. But I've learned to compensate. Now my upper body is in pretty good shape.

When I'm sitting, Angelica kneels beside me. She hands me one end of an elastic therapy cord. I grip the two handles while she keeps hold of the other end. Slowly, I tilt backward. It's a helpless feeling, like a skydiver in free fall. Then the cord resists, and it's like a parachute opening. But I still have to nail the landing.

"And back up," Angelica says.

Gritting my teeth, I struggle to return to the seated position. "See?" I say breathlessly. "I'm doing good, right?"

"You moved about an inch. Now let's see if we can do two."

I repeat the exercise, but she doesn't look very impressed. Sure, it's partly my fault for not practicing twice a day for five minutes like I'm supposed to, but she doesn't seem to realize how incredibly *tiring* this is. Being a qualified PT isn't the same as being paraplegic.

"All right," she says. "Onto your belly."

I roll over. Angelica helps to lift me at the waist, so I'm propped up on my forearms and knees. "Let's start with a plank kick down," she says.

That's another annoying thing about PT: there's a lot of jargon, and it's impossible to keep the exercises straight in my head. Okay, yes, I'd probably remember the names better if I worked out at home, but I'm busy. Minecraft cities don't just build themselves, you know.

I think she's lifting my ankles, but it's hard to tell—I really don't have any feeling down there. It's like my brain is sending signals, but they're getting lost halfway.

"And . . . kick down," she says.

I try to do as she says, but I honestly don't know if anything's happening. I can't even see my feet when I'm in this position. I'm propped up like a paralyzed pet porcupine, pretending I have a clue what my body is doing. It makes me want to scream.

"Okay," she says. "Let's get back to a sitting position."

She helps me shuffle around, which takes way longer than it probably should. At least it gives me time to take ten slow breaths. Slow breathing is a relaxation technique she taught me—I use it to stop myself from spontaneously combusting during incredibly frustrating PT sessions.

When I'm finally seated before her, Angelica points to my socked feet. This time I know what she wants and I stare hard, willing my toes to move. *Slow and steady, Noah. Just stay cool.*

"Tell me when you're ready to start," Angelica says.

"I already did!" I snap.

She nods, but her tone is firm. "If you want things to get better, Noah, you've got to put in the work. Just look at Dynamo."

She points across the room, where the mighty Dynamo has progressed to the treadmill. Strapped into his weight-supporting harness, he puffs and pants his way to a depressingly slow walk.

I resist the urge to point out that he gets winded after ten steps, and that he has the world's stupidest Mohawk. Dynamo is every PT's favorite charity case because he's willing to humiliate himself publicly. "He's certainly an impressive specimen," I say.

Angelica tsks. "Don't be sarcastic."

I should really keep my mouth shut, but . . . *Oh, whatever.* "I'm totally serious," I say in my most chipper voice. "I secretly hope that when I grow up, I'll be as cool as him!"

She pulls a face. "Positive remarks only, please."

Dynamo's PT winds down the treadmill, which doesn't take long, as it's hardly moving. Then she passes him a towel. Dynamo runs it across his forehead like a prizefighter after ten rounds in the ring and flings it back to her. He's ready to walk another three yards, I guess.

Go, Dynamo!

"You don't need to be jealous of him," Angelica says.

I stare at her. "You don't actually think I'm *jealous* of Dynamo, do you?"

She tilts her head to one side. "I think you lack confidence."

"Unlike Dynamo, who *should* lack confidence but doesn't."

"He's a good kid."

"He has a Mohawk."

"I think it looks cool," she says.

"Are you kidding? He probably only has it to hide how short he is."

"He says his girlfriend likes it."

I bust out laughing. "Wait . . . *girlfriend*? He's *nine*! And he looks like a toilet brush."

"Maybe she likes that."

"Maybe she's blind. That'd help."

"You're being very negative, Noah."

"I'm positive you're right," I say.

Angelica huffs. When she started working with me four months ago, she used to laugh when I said something witty. Now she looks like she wishes she'd been assigned to toilet-brush boy. "Listen, have you thought about seeing a counselor again?" she asks.

I tense up. "Why would I want to do that?"

She sighs deeply. "Noah, please."

I don't know if she's saying, *Noah, please see a counselor*, or *Noah, please stop pretending you don't understand*. Doesn't matter. I don't want to have this conversation.

"Do you know why we do PT?" she asks finally.

"PT seeks to rehabilitate through specially designed exercises," I reply in a singsong voice.

"Yes." Her eyebrows crinkle like she's thinking hard. "In fact, that's the exact definition in the handbook I gave you. You read it a lot, huh?"

Actually, I just remember that one sentence, because I thought "rehabilitate" meant *fix*. Even "specially designed exercises" sounded scientific, like there was a magic formula to undo what happened to me. After two months as a full-time resident of the Children's Hospital, I discovered there's no magic formula. After two more months as an outpatient,

I'm embarrassed that I ever thought there was.

"Reading's not the problem," I say coolly. "My eyes and brain work just fine. It's the rest of my body that's messed up."

Mom wouldn't like my tone of voice. Neither would Dad, if he were still alive. I wonder if Angelica will call me on it. *Maybe you'd do better if you spent time exercising instead of reading, Noah.* Or: *Isn't it time for an attitude adjustment, Noah?*

Instead, she nods like she understands. "I've told you, there's no reason you can't regain some use of your legs. But PT is a marathon, not a sprint. The only way to progress is to take a step . . . and then another and another. Take enough steps, and you'll finish any race. Even this one."

I've heard all this stuff before. Usually I just blow it off. But not this time. "What does that mean?" I demand. "What *race?*"

"Your journey," she says.

"A journey's not a race."

"Okay. Then let's call it a journey."

I can feel myself tensing up with every word. Race, journey—doesn't matter. It's all just words. "How long will this *journey* take?"

"Well," she explains patiently, "that's up to you."

24

"So, if I want to finish today, I can?"

"I think you know that's not realistic."

"How will I know when I reach the end? What does 'some use of my legs' even mean?"

"Every person's recovery is different. But there's no substitute for courage and hard work."

I feel like a volcano that's about to erupt. Before the accident, I didn't need courage to stand up, or walk across the room, or slide onto a toilet seat. But everything changed in the blink of an eye. And all the hard work in the world won't fix me. If it could, I'd be playing baseball again and Dynamo would be competing in the Olympics instead of slogging along in a weight-supporting harness just like he was when I started PT. And maybe nine year olds with toilet brush hair can believe in a winnable marathon—heck, most nine-year-olds will worship the Easter Bunny just as long as it keeps bringing them candy—but I'm not nine, and I'm not stupid. I don't think I'm ever getting out of this wheelchair, and when I look around me, I don't see a bunch of winners. I just see people who can't face up to the fact they've already lost.

Angelica watches me. She doesn't need to be a mind reader to see that I'm angry. Furious, even. She's probably thinking this would be a perfect opportunity for us to explore the world of *feelings*. She's probably right too. It'd feel so good to tell her what I really think of PT. Anything to beat back the tears that are building behind my eyes.

But when I open my mouth, my voice is small and defeated. "I'll try to work harder on the exercises this week," I say.

Several seconds pass before she replies. "This is the first week of the rest of your life, Noah. Let's make it count, okay?"

Then she flashes a glimmer of a smile that looks as empty as I feel.

THE FIRST HOUR OF THE FIRST WEEK
OF THE REST OF MY LIFE

f PT is bad, getting into our minivan afterward might be
even worse. It has a five-star crash-test rating and more
than enough space for a wheelchair. Unfortunately, it's not
wheelchair accessible, because wheelchair conversions cost
at least ten thousand dollars, and we don't have ten grand
hiding out in Mom's piggy bank. Which means that it takes
about five minutes to get me on board.

Mom meets me in the parking garage. She opens the
side-door panel, wraps her arms around me, and hoists me
up. Staggering sideways, she dumps me into the van. Even
though I'm pretty short and skinny as a rail, this process

involves a lot of grunting, and not much of it is coming from me. The heavy lifting isn't getting any easier for Mom, probably because the object being lifted is still growing.

Luckily, I can support myself once I'm in my seat. While I buckle up, Mom heads to the back. She folds my wheelchair and places it carefully inside. The whole van dips a little as she slams the rear door. Then she climbs into the driver's seat, sucking deep breaths like she's been working out—which I guess she has been.

"So," she says, starting the engine, "how did it go?"

"Great," I say. "Unbelievable progress."

She watches me in the rearview mirror. "Really?"

"Sure."

"Honestly?"

"Well, kind of."

Her eyes drift back to the garage ramp. "Not so good, then, huh?"

"Not great, no."

This is what our conversations are like these days: little lies to hide the truth we don't want to share. It's pointless, but it's a habit now, like we don't know how else to talk.

Mom is the youngest of six children. Her brothers and sisters called her "Runt." She likes to say she grew up with a quiet mouth and a black belt in conflict avoidance. Me, I'm an only child, but my mouth isn't so quiet, and I don't have a black belt in anything.

We pull onto Children's Place and then join the rush-hour traffic on Kingshighway Boulevard.

"Okay if I reheat leftovers for dinner?" Mom asks. "It's your favorite, lasagna."

"Great."

"Yeah." She shuffles in her seat. "And, uh, I thought I'd head out for a while this evening, okay?"

"After dinner?"

She hesitates. "Before."

She's not exactly *lying*, but Mom is definitely hiding something. "Where are you going?" I ask.

"Just, you know, to a restaurant."

"On your own?"

"No. With Mr. Dillon."

"The guy down the street?"

"Yeah."

A thought occurs to me. "Didn't his wife run off with another man?"

She massages the steering wheel. "You know perfectly well she did. The poor man's still getting over it. That's why I

29

thought it would be nice for us to chat."

I don't like where this conversation is going. "Why would he want to talk to *you*?"

Mom makes a little sound at the back of her throat. "You're right, Noah. Why would anyone want to talk to *me*?"

More silence. We've reached the truth, and neither of us likes how it feels.

"It's just dinner," she says.

I watch enough TV to know that for grown-ups, "dinner" is a code word for *date*.

"Kathy's going to pop round to check on you," she adds, like a visit from our elderly neighbor and her loose-fitting teeth is a special treat. "Please don't make this hard for me, Noah. *Please*."

I can't stand seeing Mom like this, so I say what I have to say. "Okay."

She stops at a red light and turns to face me. "Thank you," she says. Then she breathes out deeply, like she's letting go of all her worry.

I don't think either of us is really happy, though. Agreeing not to argue isn't the same as getting along.

HOW TO RUIN MY FAVORITE FOOD

We live in a neighborhood called The Hill. A hundred years ago, a bunch of Italians (including my great-great-grandfather) came to St. Louis, and pretty much all of them settled here. They called it The Hill because it's built on a hill, which goes to show how imaginative our ancestors were.

Our house is a bungalow: two bedrooms, one bathroom, kitchen and living room, all on one floor. Maybe that sounds small, but most of the houses around here are shotgun style, long and narrow, so it could be worse—I have enough trouble getting my wheelchair around the furniture as it is.

While Mom gets ready for her dinner-that-isn't-really-a-date, I do my homework on the small kitchen table. The work isn't difficult, but there's a lot of it. For a start, there are thirty math problems, and none of them is about baseball.

Our geriatric dachshund, Flub, jumps onto my lap while I'm working. This is yet another downside to being in a wheelchair—I'm like an elevated dog bed. Flub turns around and around, kneading my legs like dough, until eventually he settles back where he started. Warm and comfortable at last, he makes a special delivery: a silent but violent fluffy that makes me gag. With his nose jammed tight between my legs, the freaking dog probably can't even smell it.

Mom chooses this moment to join me in the kitchen. She's wearing a dark-blue dress and red lipstick. I haven't seen her looking like this since Dad died.

"You feeling all right?" she asks, sniffing the air.

"It was Flub," I say.

"Oh." She takes a deep breath, and then looks like she wishes she hadn't.

I guess I should just come out and say it. Another really delightful part of my life in a Corvette wheelchair is that I don't have complete control over my downstairs plumbing. Because of that, Mom is in the habit of checking to see if

I'm "okay." It's absolutely as awesome as you'd think. What almost-twelve-year-old wouldn't want his mom keeping track of his pee and poop patterns?

Mom must be feeling guilty about abandoning me because she takes the plate of lasagna from the fridge and reheats it in the microwave. She doesn't usually do that. The occupational therapists at Children's helped her reorganize the kitchen so that I could reach everything from my wheelchair, and ever since then, Mom has been tough on me about being self-sufficient.

As the plate spins, she watches the clock, as nervous as a batter facing Logan Montgomery in a Little League game.

"So, what's Mr. Dillon like?" I ask her.

She plays with her dress collar. "You know what he's like. You used to see him at the bus stop when you were in elementary school. His daughter's Makayla, remember?"

"She was in second grade."

"And now she's in fourth."

"But what's he *like*?" I ask again.

She chews the inside of her cheek. "He's nice. He saw me unloading groceries last week and . . . Well, we got talking, and he asked if I'd like to have dinner sometime."

I wait for the rest of the story, but I guess that's all there is. "You're telling me this date is all because he helped you *unload groceries?*"

"For Pete's sake, Noah, it's not a date!" She hands me a knife and fork. "Anyway, I just thought it would be nice to go out for once. You know, talk to someone."

"You can talk to me."

"I mean a grown-up."

"What about your friends?"

Mom purses her lips. "I just want to talk to someone who—"

The microwave timer interrupts her with a loud ding. She takes out the plate and places it on the table next to my homework. I wonder if she's going to finish her thought, but I'm not sure I want to know where she was going. Someone who . . . is *male? Single?*

I remember the last time she wore the blue dress. It was her store's Christmas party. Dad was wearing his smart gray suit, his hair combed super carefully to make it seem like he wasn't so bald after all. Not that he was embarrassed about his hair—he just liked to make the best of every situation.

Like, Dad was always the first parent onto the field after every Little League game. And he always congratulated everyone, even if we lost. And whenever Coach Montgomery chewed his son out in the middle of a game, Dad was always the one leading a cheer for Logan. Not that it ever helped. Logan still picked on me.

"Eat up," Mom says, interrupting my thoughts.

I'm not really hungry, but I don't want her to feel bad, so I load up my fork. I ought to blow on it, but Flub's nose has apparently been reactivated, and as he unearths his snout from between my legs and extends his tongue about six inches, I imagine the entire dinner ending up in his stomach. So I gobble the forkful in a single bite.

Big mistake.

"Be careful," Mom says. "It's hot."

She fills a glass with water and hands it to me so that I can douse my burning mouth. The way she keeps handling things to me makes me feel like a little kid, unable to do anything for myself. I hate it, especially because I can still remember when things were so different. When I'd just walk to the sink and stick my mouth under the faucet. Now, I can hardly reach the tap.

It's strange all the tiny ways life changes when your butt is stuck in a chair.

The doorbell rings. Mom runs her hands down her dress like she's trying to iron out the wrinkles and goes to answer the door. Flub slithers off my lap, lands with a thud on the linoleum floor, and expresses his discomfort with a full-bodied fart.

I take another bite of lasagna, but it doesn't taste right. Usually, it's dense with ricotta and about twenty other cheeses I can't spell, but tonight it mostly tastes dry.

I hear Flub barking and Mom and Mr. Dillon greeting each other. Their footsteps clatter against the hardwood floors as they follow the hallway to the kitchen. When he sees me, Mr. Dillon strides over and shakes my hand. He has a strong grip and large fingers that look especially dark against my pasty white skin. "It's good to see you again, Noah," he says.

He's got a smile a mile wide and a belly to match. I don't think he's as big as Double-Wide, but he definitely eats more lasagna than I do.

"Hmm-hmm," I reply. Then I see Mom looking hopeful and anxious, so I add, "You too."

As Mom smiles, Mr. Dillon sniffs the air meaningfully.

"It was the dog," I say.

"Oh."

For a few seconds, we're all as still as statues, waiting for someone to make the situation less awkward than it obviously is.

"So," Mom says, "does the, uh, lasagna taste okay?"

The honest answer is no. But I'm not sure the problem is with the food, and I don't want to get into an argument with Mom when the real issue is standing right next to us, so I say, "It's great."

She isn't convinced. Mom has learned the meaning of my every look, word, and silence, and she knows something is up now.

"You go enjoy your fancy dinner," I say.

Now she looks even more worried. She'd probably bail on Mr. Dillon if I pushed a little, but then I'd be the one feeling guilty instead of her.

"Seriously, Mom, I'm good."

Nodding, Mom walks over and kisses me on the cheek. Then she tears off a piece of paper towel and uses it to wipe away the lipstick print. Did I say she was making me feel like a little kid? Scratch that—I feel like a baby.

"Kathy will pop in soon to check on you," she says.

"Awesome," I reply in my most un-awesome voice.

"And you know my number."

"Yes," I say. "I know your number."

"And I can come back if you need me."

"In that new invention they're calling the automobile."

"Don't be cheeky," she says, forcing a smile.

"And don't be late," I shoot back. "I'd really hate to ground you."

Mom chuckles. Mr. Dillon is still flashing his pearly-white smile like an actor in a toothpaste commercial. I'd give anything to wipe that smug look off his face.

"All right, then," Mom says.

She turns and leaves the kitchen. Mr. Dillon trails after her. Ten seconds later, the front door opens and closes and I'm alone, wondering why lying is sometimes the only way to make someone feel better.

I push the lasagna away. Push the math homework away. Roll backward and wheel myself around the table and past the appliances. Once I'm across the hallway and into the living room I start up Mom's old desktop computer and play Minecraft.

Within seconds, I'm building an entirely new world—one with the soaring towers of downtown St. Louis and awesome views across the Mississippi River. And the more I add, the more I leave behind all the things I don't want in the real world: Logan Montgomery and baseball, Dynamo Duric and physical therapy. And most of all, Mr. Dillon and any version of my mother that would date him.

PE IS NOT MY FRIEND

Wellspring Middle School has alternating schedules for A and B days, which means that the next day, Tuesday, is a PE day. And PE means quality time with Mrs. Friendly.

Unfortunately, Mrs. Friendly is not very friendly. If I had to teach middle school PE, I wouldn't be very friendly either, but she's an ex-marine, so she's been trained to be angry. She's also the nearest thing our school has to a celebrity, because she spends her summers doing CrossFit competitions on TV.

No one messes with Mrs. Friendly.

On day one of seventh grade, Mrs. Friendly spoke to my

mom and said, "I want your son to be involved. Do you want your son to be involved? Or do you want him to sit on the sidelines and watch?" What she was really saying was: "I like to torment students. Do you want me to torment your son too? Or do you want him to be an outcast?"

If I'd been around for this conversation, I would've told Mom that being an outcast actually makes a whole lot of sense. For example, outcasts don't get hurt. But Mom is scared of Mrs. Friendly because Mom is smart, so apparently she just nodded and said, "Whatever you think is best."

That's why I'm sitting in my wheelchair in the middle of the gym, watching Logan Montgomery warming up for a massive kick at home plate. I can't believe we're still playing kickball in middle school, but Mrs. Friendly is all about competition and team building. Logan is not on my team, but I'm pretty sure he's determined to kick the ball to me, just to see if I can still catch.

"You okay?" Double-Wide asks from behind me.

I crane my neck around to look at him. Wisely, he has taken up the farthest fielding position in the gym. He's so far from home plate, he could take a step backward and leave the gym completely.

"I'm fine," I say.

This is a lie. I am not fine. I'm thinking about how Mom was smiling when she got home last night. I haven't seen her crack a smile in months, but a couple hours with Mr. Dillon and she's happy again. I am absolutely *not* okay with Mom having a boyfriend. It's bad enough that she makes me do PE.

Alyssa, our team's pitcher, is preparing to roll the ball toward Logan. He has a crazy smile on his face, like the villain in a comic strip.

"Why is Logan looking at you like that?" Double-Wide asks me.

"It's complicated," I say.

"Why?"

I'm trying to focus on sending negative vibes to Mr. Dillon, but Double-Wide won't stop until I answer. "We used to play on the same Little League team."

"You played *baseball*?" he exclaims. "With *Logan*?"

"I was the starting catcher."

"No way!"

I whip my chair around. "Yes way! And if you must know, I was pretty good. They called me Velcro, because pitches stuck to my glove."

"Cool." Double-Wide scratches his neck. "What did you use to make the ball stick?"

"Nothing! It's just what you say when a catcher never drops the ball."

He probably has more questions, but just then I hear Logan kick the ball. Gripping the high-pressure tires, I spin around and zone in on the ball—just in time to get an up-close view as it beans me.

It's a full-facial hit. Literally, not an inch of my face escapes the inflated rubber. For a split second, it compresses to follow the contours of my nose and cheeks and lips. Because my mouth is open, a few molecules probably even touch my tongue.

For how many years have middle school students been touching this ball? How many times has it rolled across the dirty gym floor? How many times has it been kicked by sneakers that have traces of dog poop on them?

How much of that dirt and dog poop is now on my face? And in my mouth?

"Are you okay?" Double-Wide asks.

I'm too embarrassed to answer that. Plus, I can't stop thinking about the poop. My saliva tastes really weird.

Alyssa stands alone in the pitcher's circle. She has this pitying look, like she's watching a movie of a stranded baby sea lion.

I am *not* a stranded baby sea lion.

"Next play, Savino," says Mrs. Friendly. "Just focus on the next play."

Next play?! Is she kidding? My spit tastes of middle school germs and sneaker poop. And my nose hurts too.

Logan skips around the bases and slides into home plate like he's scoring the winning run in game seven of the World Series. His teammates help him up, and they all bump fists. In contrast, my teammates do not rush over and congratulate me. They do not bump my fist. Heck, they won't even look at me. It's like they're pretending nothing happened. As if they haven't just witnessed the most humiliating thing in the entire history of middle school PE.

Alyssa glares at Logan. Logan flicks his head casually and grins right back at her. Winning never gets old for Logan.

"Why did you slide?" Alyssa calls out to him.

The gym gets a little quieter. Logan shrugs. "Why shouldn't I?"

"You were showboating. In a real game, the pitcher would aim the next ball at your body."

"Lucky you're not a real pitcher, then, isn't it?"

His teammates reward him with cheers, but only until

Alyssa begins striding toward him. "You think you're so special, huh?"

"I scored on you, didn't I?"

Alyssa snorts. "In *kickball.*"

"Like you'd be better off playing baseball!"

"Why don't we find out?"

Alyssa has never liked Logan, but she's also never been crazy enough to go toe-to-toe with him at home plate either. Now she's caught him off guard. He shoots a curious look at Mrs. Friendly like he's waiting for her to intervene. But like I say, Mrs. Friendly is all about competition, even when there are no TV cameras.

For the first time in as long as I can remember, Logan seems on edge. He frowns, but then the swagger is back and he begins to laugh. "Whatever," he says.

"What are you afraid of?" Alyssa growls. "Losing? Or losing to a *girl*?"

It's the "girl" part that gets to him. Logan's never backed down from a fight in his life—heck, he's started most of them—and he can't give in to Alyssa now. It's not in his DNA.

"Fine," he says. "You're on."

"Good." With her fists jammed against her hips, Alyssa looks like an outlaw from a Wild West movie. "Tomorrow, lunchtime. I pitch to you. You pitch to me. Whoever gets the out wins."

"And who's going to catch, huh?" Logan asks, once it's clear he's not getting out of the arrangement. "Or did you forget that part?"

Alyssa looks over her shoulder, and her eyes find me. I shake my head, but it's too late. Alyssa has a plan, and I'm in it.

"Noah," she says. "He'll be perfect."

SMALL PORTIONS

At lunch on Wednesday, Double-Wide seems worried. "This isn't a lot of food," he says, eyeing the calorie-controlled portion.

"No," I agree, "it's not. But once you've tasted it, you might be grateful they don't give you much."

He tugs at the collar of his rust-colored polo shirt. "That bad, huh?"

"Let's just say, the meat comes straight from PetSmart."

"Seriously?"

I sigh. "No. Not really."

Even if he doesn't appreciate my major league–level sarcasm

skills, I'm glad to have Double-Wide around, especially at lunchtime. Alyssa's been sitting with me most days since I broke away from the baseball posse, but I sometimes wonder if she's doing it for the same reason Mrs. Friendly makes me do PE: she doesn't want me to be an outcast.

Double-Wide and I make a beeline for the farthest corner of the cafeteria because it's a safe distance from Logan. A couple minutes later, Alyssa grabs her lunch and heads toward us.

"Noah," begins Double-Wide, "are you and Alyssa . . . you know . . . together?"

"*Together?*" I say. "No! We're just friends."

Actually, it's a little more complicated than that. Alyssa always had my back in elementary school, especially when Logan mouthed off at me. But when I started hanging out with the team in sixth grade, things changed. One day she caught me smiling as Logan picked on a teammate, and I could see she was shocked. I wanted to explain that I wasn't smiling because it was funny. I was just grateful that he wasn't picking on me for a change. But I was ashamed to admit I never stood up for myself, so I kept quiet. After that, it got harder to talk to Alyssa about other things too.

Anyway, it's not like she didn't have lots else going on last year. She joined a book club and started taking photographs for the yearbook. In the spring, she got moved up a grade for Language Arts, so we saw even less of each other. But after my accident, she was the first person from school to visit me in the hospital. She came by most days after that too, and it was like being back in elementary school, riding the bus together, just talking. I like being friends with her again.

But real friends don't rope their disabled friends into catching pitches delivered by a hulking nemesis with an arm like a cannon.

Not that Alyssa is showing any signs of remorse. She pulls up a chair and nods at me, all smiles. "Hey, Noah. Hey, Ruben."

"Please, call me Double-Wide," he says.

"Uh . . ."

"Or Dee-Dub. My dad came up with that. Says it sounds better."

"Dee-Dub?" I ask.

"Yeah. It's short for D-W. You know, the abbreviation for Double-Wide."

Alyssa wears the frozen smile of someone trying to make nice with a grizzly bear. "O-okay . . . *Dee-Dub*."

As she spreads a napkin neatly across her lap, Dee-Dub and I tuck in to our soggy burgers and smashed potatoes.

We each have precisely three carrot sticks too. Maybe there's a world carrot stick shortage so the school has to ration us.

"Do you always use a napkin?" Dee-Dub asks Alyssa.

She nods. "Helps to keep my clothes stain free." She waves her hands across her chest like a game-show hostess unveiling tonight's grand prize: a black-and-yellow striped T-shirt. Then she stops suddenly. "Are you checking out my boobs again, Noah?"

My eyes shoot upward. "What? No! I was looking at your T-shirt."

"It's a very nice T-shirt," Dee-Dub agrees. "Makes you look like a bumblebee."

Alyssa sighs. "So, tell me about Albuquerque. That's where you came from, right?"

Dee-Dub nods. "Well, there's a lot of desert. It's not humid like it is here. It's not as green either."

"Do you miss it?"

"I don't know."

"You don't know?" Alyssa tries to stab a carrot with her fork but ends up chasing it around the plate. "What about your friends? You must miss them."

Dee-Dub stares at his half-eaten burger. "I didn't have a lot of friends."

"Oh." Alyssa makes eye contact with me as if this is *news*. Me, I'm not surprised at all. Dee-Dub says weird stuff, he's huge, and he wears odd clothes. He's like the Bermuda Triangle of impossibility, the trifecta of terribleness: strange, big, uncool.

But you know what? It really doesn't matter. Because as I scope out the cafeteria, I'm pretty sure there are still more people gawking at me than at him.

Sometimes you don't need the trifecta. One thing—just *one thing*—can be enough to make sure you stand out. And getting roped into a baseball game with Logan and Alyssa definitely isn't going to help.

The crazy thing is, she only challenged Logan to get back at him for the kickball fiasco. Doesn't she realize that when he unleashes his vicious fastball or smacks her pitch with his powerful swing, we'll end up looking even more pathetic?

I put down my plastic fork. "This pitch-off is a bad idea."

"This pitch-off," Alyssa replies, giving me a hard stare, "is *justice*. If no one stands up to Logan, he'll never learn."

By "no one," I figure she means *me*. "Well, I don't think getting humiliated is going to teach us much. And you never should've said I'd play catcher."

"Who else was I supposed to pick? Logan's teammates

would cheat so that he wins."

"I don't think they'd need to cheat for that to happen," says Dee-Dub.

She scowls at him, but it looks fake. If anything, she seems to find the idea of losing kind of funny. Which is very confusing. And suspicious.

"Trust me, Noah," she says. "This is going to be fun."

"Fun" isn't the word I'd use, and it shouldn't be the word she uses either. But what Alyssa lacks in baseball experience, she more than makes up for in smarts.

And as Mom is always reminding me: brains can be dangerous too.

PITCHING A FIT

I f my life were a movie, the director would fast-forward twenty minutes to Logan and Alyssa's pitch-off. Viewers would find me in my wheelchair on the blacktop, warming up by catching lightning quick fastballs. They'd think, *Wow, Noah got outside really quickly!* Or maybe they wouldn't think about the whole getting-outside thing at all.

Unfortunately, my life is not a movie.

In reality, this is what happens: I reverse from the cafeteria table, rotate ninety degrees, and begin my tortuous journey through the labyrinth of scattered chairs. From time to time, I bump into one, and the chair leg squeaks loudly against the tile floor and kids look up accusingly. When they realize the perpetrator is me, they look away again quickly. And the whole time, Alyssa hovers nearby. I can tell she wants to help, but she knows I have to do this alone.

It doesn't get much better when we leave the cafeteria. The elevator is only ten yards away, but it's ancient, and Murphy's Law says it's stuck on one of the other floors. Dee-Dub taps his foot impatiently as we wait. When the door finally opens, he says, "Twenty-five seconds. That's remarkably slow."

No kidding.

Wellspring Middle School was built almost a hundred years ago, back when people thought it was a good idea for schools to have three floors and a flight of ten steep concrete steps leading to the ornate main entrance . . . on the second floor. This means I spend a lot of time in the elevator and even more time waiting for it.

Alyssa and Dee-Dub aren't allowed to ride with me, so I have to take the half-minute journey to the first floor alone. When the doors finally open, I find Alyssa and Dee-Dub staring at their watches like they're afraid time has stalled. I often wonder the same thing myself.

On the bright side, it's only twenty yards, two wheelchair ramps, and one electric door until we're outside, where the real punishment can begin.

We might have a fancy main entrance, but like most St. Louis Public Schools, Wellspring Middle doesn't have a field, so Logan waits for us on the blacktop. While Alyssa warms up her arm, I wheel over to him.

"Uh, Logan," I say in a voice that sounds higher than usual, "my PT says I'm not allowed to, you know, catch baseballs."

"Whatever." He reaches into the bag at his feet and pulls out a catcher's mask and glove. "You'll be safe with these."

A crowd is gathering. I can't tell if they're here for the competition or because they want to see me get beaned again—with a real baseball this time! I really want to leave, but I don't want to let Alyssa down.

Sweat runs into my eyes behind the smelly mask. It's sweltering on the blacktop. As he shuffles over, Dee-Dub seems to be suffering even more than me.

"Are those gargoyles?" he asks, pointing to the corners of the old brick building.

"Believe it or not, yes," I say. "You should see them when it rains."

"Why?"

"Five years ago, some of the graduating class climbed on the roof and rerouted the gutters. Now the rainwater sprays out from between the gargoyles' legs. Nothing says 'Welcome to Wellspring' like a whizzing gargoyle, you know."

"You two done making out yet?" Logan shouts. "Let's get this started."

Logan wins the coin toss and pitches first. Standing in the middle of the blacktop, right arm raised, left leg cocked, he uncoils his body and whips the baseball right at me. Alyssa swings the bat with a satisfying but useless swoosh, and the ball embeds itself in my glove.

"Stee-rike!" yells Logan, pumping his fist in the air.

My bones feel like they've been crushed. Still, I'm surprised at how natural it felt to catch the ball.

"Remind me how this is going to punish Logan?" I stage-whisper to Alyssa.

"Shh! I'm concentrating."

I toss the ball back to Logan, but my aim is way off. He runs to retrieve it. "At least you can still catch!" he shouts. "Well, except in kickball."

Alyssa gives me a warning look. "Ignore him," she says. "We let our play do the talking."

I seriously doubt that, but I nod anyway. I'm definitely feeling motivated to up my game. If I don't, I might get pasted again. I wonder which is worse: getting hit by a solid object at high speed or by a poop-smeared rubber kickball.

Logan winds up and pitches a laserlike fastball that's in my glove before Alyssa even begins her swing.

"Strike two!" Logan crows.

Alyssa takes the ball from me and lobs it back to him. She seems very relaxed for someone who's about to be struck out on consecutive pitches.

Logan's about to throw the same pitch again. I can see it in his eyes. I bet Alyssa can see it too. Trouble is, she doesn't stand a chance of hitting it.

Sure enough, he flings the ball, and she swings the bat, and like opposing magnets, the two never meet. The pitch is so high it wouldn't be called a strike, but she has swung and missed.

"Strikeout!" Logan blows on his hand like he's trying to cool it off.

Alyssa hands me the bat. "My turn," she says.

Dee-Dub sidles up to me. "Has Alyssa ever batted before?" he asks. "Because I've got to say, she really whiffed."

He retreats as Logan jogs over to me and takes the bat. "You can relax now, Savino," Logan says. "I'm not going to let this ball get anywhere near your glove."

He gets into his batter's stance, knees slightly bent, bat

raised over his right shoulder. The crowd is large now, and Logan loves it. Even Mrs. Friendly has emerged from inside the building to watch the duel. It's like she's got radar that detects athletic competition within a mile radius.

As Alyssa winds up, Logan adjusts his grip. He's usually impatient at the plate—it's his biggest weakness—but not today. He's so confident, he doesn't even twitch a muscle until Alyssa releases the ball. He wants to get a read on it. End this contest with a single swing.

The ball flies from her hand quicker than I expect, but it's on a collision course with the blacktop. Logan doesn't swing because he doesn't need to. He just watches as it lands a yard in front of him, ricochets off the ground, shoots up, and cracks against the outside of his left knee.

Logan drops the bat and grabs his knee. Hops up and down on his right leg, growling something strange and definitely rude.

"Oopsy!" Alyssa calls out.

Logan, tired of hopping, lowers his left leg and tries to put weight on it. Which is not a good idea, because he topples over and lands on his hip.

"Arrrgh!" he screams, rolling around. "What the heck!"

As Logan's shocked teammates watch their fallen leader,

Dee-Dub crouches beside me. "That was a surprisingly effective pitch," he says.

"Sure was," I reply.

I figure Alyssa will be giving high fives to everyone in sight, but she isn't. She's a picture of innocence as she watches Logan writhing on the ground.

But as she turns away and heads for the school building, she looks over at Dee-Dub and me. And in the moment before she goes inside, she winks.

She actually *winks*.

"Wow," I say. "I think Alyssa took out Logan on purpose."

"She's like a black-and-yellow-striped ninja assassin," says Dee-Dub admiringly. "I advise that we stay on her good side from now on."

That might just be the most sensible thing he's said.

DOUBLING DOWN

After school, I sit outside the main entrance and wait for Mom to pick me up. She's not usually late, and it's still baking hot. I can't complain, though. She could make me take the school bus to and from school, which would mean waking up half an hour earlier every day. Since school starts at seven a.m. and I'm a big fan of sleep, that would be a disaster.

So here I am, roasting in my black wheelchair, sweat pooling around my butt, when Logan emerges from the school. As usual, he's not alone.

"Noah!" He grunts my name like it's a cuss word and hobbles over. There's a big red welt on the outside of his left knee.

"Did you tell Alyssa to do this to me?"

I put on a confused face. "Do *what* to you, Logan?"

"Try to break my leg."

"Nope." I press my lips tight together. "I told her to aim for your balls."

Logan's teammates snicker but shut up real quick when he glares at them.

"Hi, Logan!" Alyssa calls out. "Are you feeling any better?"

Logan, teeth gritted, watches her wheel her bike toward us. She has spray-painted the frame matte black, but the mean-machine look is undone by the star-spangled tassels dangling from the handlebars. At least her bright-yellow helmet color coordinates with her bumblebee T-shirt.

"Seems like you and me have some unfinished business, Choo," he mutters.

"You and *I*," she says, correcting him. "Grammar is so important, Logan. Especially now that your baseball career is over."

Logan makes a strange growling sound. "You're pathetic. You didn't even *try* to win fair."

"The way I see it," she says, "a tie is like a win."

"A *tie*? You *hit* me! That's an automatic base."

"But you didn't touch first base."

"Because there wasn't one!"

"An oversight, for sure," she agrees.

Logan's teammates know better than to laugh again, but I can't help myself. Logan eyeballs me, but I still can't stop. I don't know if Alyssa has a future in baseball, but when it comes to a battle of wits, she's schooling Logan.

"If you'd given me a real pitch," Logan spits, "I would've hit it out of the city."

Alyssa frowns. "On one leg?"

"I wouldn't *be* on one leg if you hadn't struck me."

"I don't think it was technically a strike. But it was certainly an effective pitch, if I do say so myself."

Logan is literally hopping mad now. "I want a rematch!" he shouts.

Alyssa looks like she's caught a whiff of a Flub special. "Why would I do that?"

"You won't," he sneers. "'Cause you're a joke with a loud mouth and no arm!"

For a moment, there's total silence. Logan has always been hot-tempered—his competitive streak is so strong that almost everything boils down to winning and losing—but this time he has crossed a line.

"Back off, Logan," I say, wheeling between them. I crane

my neck to make eye contact. He looks especially big up close. "You got hit by a pitch. Happens all the time in the big leagues. Not that you'd know anything about that."

He snorts. "Says the kid who can't even play."

My hands are shaking. "Oh, yeah? So, how'd last season go without me catching for you?"

I can tell by his reaction that I've hit a nerve. I wonder what annoys Logan more: that his Little League team lost more games once I stopped playing for them or that his pitching was part of the problem.

"You think you're that important, huh?" he fires back. "Then let's have a rematch. Maybe your amazing catching can help your girlfriend pitch straight."

I turn red. I don't mean to. It just happens, and I can't look at Alyssa anymore. Will people think I'm trying to protect her if I back down from Logan? Will *she* think so?

"Fine," I say. "You're on. You can have your stupid rematch."

Everyone is still watching us, and no one is speaking. But as I look into the stunned faces of my former teammates blinking against the bright sunshine, I get the feeling they're not all on Logan's side anymore. Justin and Carlos even turn away, shaking their heads.

"You better start practicing, Choo," Logan says as he lopes

away, his posse in dribs and drabs behind him.

I peer up at Alyssa. "I'm sorry," I say. "I—I didn't mean for that to happen."

She flicks the brake levers on her bike. "It was a little cruel of you, Noah," she murmurs. "I mean, just look at the poor boy. He's got only one good leg. Imagine how he's going to feel when I hit the other one."

"You're not serious."

"How else are we going to beat him?"

"I was thinking we could try practicing. Like, a lot."

She swings a leg over her bike and clicks her helmet strap closed. "Suits me. How about Friday? Five thirty at your house."

"Uh, sure."

Are we really teaming up to take on Logan? It feels a little crazy but also kind of cool. And if we can pull it off, it'd be legendary.

"Hey, Alyssa," I say as she prepares to pedal away. "Did you hit Logan on purpose?"

She lowers both feet to the ground. "It's complicated. See, I meant to hit him, but I was aiming for his foot. The pitch kind of got away from me."

"You do know that hitting the batter is bad, right?"

"You just said it happens all the time in the major leagues."

"Well, yeah, but . . . that's different. They're retaliating. Or trying to make a point. Or . . . or something."

"I was retaliating, *and* I was making a point," she says, eyes twinkling. "And so were you when you agreed to the rematch. Now we just need to make it count."

Mom pulls up to the curb and brakes hard. She hops out of the minivan and notices that I'm not alone. "Oh, hello, Alyssa," she says.

"Hi, Mrs. Savino."

"You're not taking the bus these days?"

Alyssa raps her knuckles against the helmet. "I like fresh air." Then she stands on the pedals and sets off in the direction of her house, a couple blocks away from mine.

Mom watches her go. "I'm sorry I'm late, honey," she says. "I tried to get away, but there was a problem at the store, and—"

"It's okay, Mom. Really."

She wrings her hands, anxious to explain how guilty she feels. Me, I'm ready to get out of here. I didn't mind everyone seeing me stand up to Logan, but I'm not super excited about having spectators as I get bundled into our minivan.

I glance over Mom's shoulder as she wraps her arms

around me. Sure enough, several pairs of eyes are trained on me. Then everyone looks away like they're ashamed for having stared. Or maybe they're just embarrassed that I noticed.

Mom heaves me into the van and shuts the panel door. Once my wheelchair is tucked away in the back, she takes her place in the driver's seat. "Thanks for understanding," she says. "I try not to be late, but I'm the assistant manager, you know? I feel bad tweaking everyone's schedules all the time."

"It's okay," I tell her, because it still beats taking the bus. Plus, if she was working, it means she wasn't hanging out with Mr. Dillon again. "Actually, I'm glad you were at the store."

She eyes me in the rearview mirror. "Where else would I be?"

I shrug. "I don't know. . . . Hanging out with Mr. Dillon, maybe."

She presses her lips into a thin line. "What's your problem with Mr. Dillon?"

I can't believe she's asking me that. Not when the answer is as obvious as the empty passenger seat beside her. I can still picture Dad sitting there. Sometimes he'd turn around and wiggle his left ear, like his entire face was made of rubber. It made me laugh when I was younger and roll my eyes when I got to middle school. But I wouldn't roll my eyes if he were here with us now. I'd wrap my arms around him and make sure he never left us.

Can Mom still picture him too?

"Please, Noah," she says. "Talk to me. Tell me what's going on."

I take a deep breath. "I just hate being left alone," I blurt out.

Okay, that's pathetic. And it's not even true. After Mom went out with Mr. Dillon the other evening, our neighbor Kathy came over and talked to me for twenty minutes before I could get rid of her. But feeling guilty is Mom's kryptonite, so I need to lay it on thick.

"I'm sorry," she says softly. "Kathy's not the greatest company these days, huh?"

"Not exactly, no. Neither is Flub."

She chuckles, which means I must be winning. So I swallow hard and smile right back.

"You deserve better company," she says.

"Definitely."

She starts the engine. "That's why Makayla's coming around this evening."

"Uh-huh. . . . Wait. *What?*"

"There's a pregame event for Cardinals employees at Busch Stadium tonight," she explains. "Mr. Dillon asked me to go with him. So I told him that Makayla should keep you company. I think you two are going to get along great!"

Mom's smile, which had morphed from sad to happy, now appears positively ecstatic.

Mine, not so much.

Just as Alyssa threw a freaky pitch this afternoon, I think Mom just dealt me a curve ball. And like Logan Montgomery, I never saw it coming.

REASONS NOT TO HAVE A
LITTLE SISTER

Makayla Dillon is in fourth grade. She tells me so almost as soon as she walks through the door. She also says she's the reigning class spelling bee champion and fastest kid in her entire grade. That's when Mr. Dillon shushes her. I don't know if it's because he doesn't approve of bragging or because he thinks I might not like hearing about girls with supercharged legs when I can't even stand up without help.

"You promise to be good, right?" he says, giving her a stern look.

Makayla rewards him with two enthusiastic thumbs-up.

"I'll be better than good, Daddy. I'll be awesome. Just like always."

Sheesh.

She stands by the window and waves as our parents leave. I hear doors being shut, followed by an engine turning over. Mr. Dillon's car sounds like it's suffering from bronchitis.

The moment they're gone, Makayla spins around. She's wearing several rows of hair beads in patriotic red, white, and blue, and they rattle every time she moves. Since Makayla never seems to stop moving, it's like she comes with her own soundtrack.

"So," she says, lips pursed, "you're supposed to make sure I get all my homework done."

"Yeah, right." I turn my wheelchair around and head for the computer, but Flub is blocking my way. I nudge him with my footrest, but he doesn't move. He does, however, unleash a bottom burp that is definitely not silent.

"Ewwww," squeals Makayla. "Excuse *you*."

"It was the dog," I say.

"Of course it was." She bounds over to me in a few steps and slaps a hand on my shoulder. "I do that too, you know. . . . Blame the dog every time I make a smelly."

"I'm not *blaming* him for anything. He's sixteen years old. He's incontinent."

"In-conti-*what*?"

"Incontinent. Means he can't control when he pees and poops."

She gazes at the lump before us. "Don't tell me. . . . I-N-C-," she begins, spelling out the word carefully, "O-N-T-I-N-E-N-T. Incontinent!"

I'm not sure what she expects. Applause? Chocolate?

"What about you?" she says. "Can you control when you pee and poop?"

I turn bright red, which she seems to find very funny. "That's none of your business."

She runs across the room and pulls a book from her pink backpack. Then she hurries back to me, the book cover turned out so that I can read it: *Gabriella Masterson and the Stolen Kiss.*

"What the heck is *that*?" I ask.

"It's the book I'm reading." She hands it to me. "It's amazing."

I flip through the thin pages and stop at random. It's the end of a chapter, and Gabriella is kissing a boy. Stolen or not, she seems to be enjoying it.

Makayla peers over my shoulder. "What is 'sucking face'?"

I snap the book shut and hand it back. "Does your dad know you're reading this?"

Clasping the book tightly in her hands, she presses it to her lips like she's Gabriella and the book is, well, a boy. "Sure. He told the librarian it was okay for me to check out young adult novels."

"Why?"

She shrugs. "I guess he got tired of me asking questions like, 'What does "sucking face" mean?'"

Flub must be getting tired of it too because he heaves himself off the floor and shuffles over to the sofa.

With him out of my way, I can finally get to the computer. One mouse click later, my alternate St. Louis appears: a perfect, pristine city without a single fourth-grade girl or incontinent dog.

"That looks cool," Makayla says, pulling up a chair beside me.

"Don't you need to read?" I ask, pointing to her book.

"*Need* to?" She shakes her head, hair beads rattling. "Not really. Anyway, I'm still stuck on the whole sucking face thing."

"It means kissing!"

"Kissing?" Makayla mulls this over. Then, just as I'm about to add the final block to my replica of the Gateway Arch, she inhales sharply. "Do you think our parents are sucking face right now?"

My hand slips and I destroy a crucial support from the left side of the arch. *"What?"*

"Well, think about it: They're way older than Gabriella and her boyfriend. And sucking face is just about all that Gabriella ever does. Well, that and getting straight A grades and saving polar bears from extinction."

"Polar bears?"

Makayla nods. "Gabriella is really busy. Mostly sucking face."

I try to repair my battered arch, but I'm distracted. It's not like Minecraft takes much concentration, but the image of Mom and Mr. Dillon kissing is now firmly imprinted on my mind, and it's not a pretty picture.

"Just think," says Makayla, draping her arm over my shoulder. "We might be brother and sister soon."

I make an involuntary gurgling sound and grab the headphones on the computer desk. They're large and padded, and when I turn the volume up really loud, I can almost imagine that Makayla isn't here at all.

Almost.

"Do you remember when we used to ride the bus together?" she shouts.

I pretend not to hear her.

"You and Alyssa used to make googly eyes at each other."

Block by block, I rebuild the Gateway Arch.

"I remember the time she told me that she secretly wanted to date you."

I pull the headphones off. "She said that?"

Makayla busts out laughing. "No! Actually, she said you were kind of annoying."

"Uh . . ."

"But don't worry. That's what Gabriella Masterson says about every boy she ends up kissing." Makayla plops her arm on my shoulder again and leans in close. "So there's still hope for you."

Flub, nestled on the sofa, belches loudly. Because of the timing, it's like he's responding to what Makayla just said and doesn't think I stand a chance at all.

"I'll tell you one thing, though," says Makayla, sighing. "You'd better get rid of the dog or you won't be sucking anyone's face."

I put the headphones back on and turn the volume up even

73

higher. I can't believe I told Mom that I didn't want to be left alone. If this evening proves anything, it's that being an only child comes with major perks.

Ten minutes with Makayla and I'm ready for a lifetime of solitude.

SCHOOLED BY A FOURTH GRADER

With headphones jammed against my head and music blaring, I don't hear the front door open. Flub does, though. He raises his snout, flaps his jowls, and shows us his missing teeth. If a burglar ever attempts to rob us, Flub will be as useful as a broken house alarm.

Mom is first to enter the living room. There's something weird about the way she's smiling, like she's ten years younger than when she went out earlier. I don't like it.

Mr. Dillon is right behind her. Makayla races over to him, and he scoops her up and squeezes her tightly. "Did you have fun, honey?" he asks.

"Sure did," she says. "Noah told me all about sucking face."

Mom's head whips around, her eyes on me like laser beams. "You did *what*?" she cries.

"Noah was worried that's what you were up to," Makayla continues. "You know, sucking each other's faces."

Mom and Mr. Dillon raise their hands at once. "No," they say in unison.

"Absolutely not!" Mr. Dillon exclaims.

"Why would you even think that?" demands Mom, shaking her head in disgust.

I feel like I'm in a TV sitcom. I need a witty comeback, but what comes out of my mouth is, "Uh . . ."

"This is so unlike you," Mom says, though I think she's mostly trying to reassure Mr. Dillon. "Saying something like that to Makayla, even as a joke . . ." She lowers her voice as if no one will hear her. "She's *nine*, Noah!"

"It's okay," says Mr. Dillon, grabbing his daughter's book bag like they can't escape fast enough. "We should probably be going, though. It's a school night."

Mom nods, but her eyes remain fixed on me. She looks completely humiliated.

I know exactly how she feels.

Makayla takes her bag from her father and swings it over

her shoulder. Just before she leaves, she peers back at me. It's like watching a tornado pause to admire the wreckage it has caused. "Well, see you later, Noah," she says.

Then, just like Alyssa on the school blacktop, she *winks*.

Before I can vow revenge, Makayla skips away. I hear her footsteps as she dances along the hallway.

Mom follows Mr. Dillon to the front door and apologizes once again for my bad influence. Then she storms back into the living room. "Well, that was awkward!"

"You don't believe that stuff she was saying, do you?" I ask.

"Where else would Makayla hear an expression like 'sucking face'?"

"It's in the book she was reading. I saw it."

"And you let her keep reading?"

"She said her dad lets her."

"That's ridiculous." Mom presses her hands against her hips. "I needed you to be responsible tonight, Noah. I needed you to watch out for Makayla. I needed you to *not* sit at the computer with headphones on, shutting out the real world, just like always."

I've got to say, I'm really missing the old Mom—the one with the black belt in conflict avoidance. This new version is totally unpredictable.

"I think you should know," she continues, "I got a call from the health insurance company. They only cover physical therapy as long as you're improving. If you don't show progress, they'll stop paying for it."

Is this what Angelica meant when she said I needed to do better? I can't believe she'd rat me out to the insurance people. She must've really wanted me to talk about my *feelings*.

"Looking on the bright side," I say, "no more PT would save us a couple hours a week."

Mom slams her fist against the wall, making me jump. "This isn't a joke, Noah!"

I haven't seen her this worked up since before the accident. But she's not the only one who's angry. "I know!" I shout. "I'm the one in a freaking wheelchair, remember?"

And just like that, the old Mom is back. She slumps against the doorframe like a deflated balloon. "I just . . ."

She lets the thought float away. A black belt cannot waste energy on a lost cause.

From the corner of my eye, I can still see my perfect Minecraft world on the computer monitor. It's so close, but it has never felt farther away. Or less real.

"You just *what*?" I ask quietly.

She breathes in through her teeth with a hissing sound. "I'm scared, honey," she says. "I'm scared they'll cut off your therapy, and you'll never get better. I'm doing everything I can to support you, but you're not holding up your end of the bargain. I guess what I'm really saying is . . . I can't do this alone anymore."

Her words hit me with the force of the poopy kickball in PE. Is she still talking about me? Or is this about Mr. Dillon now? Is that why she's hanging out with him, because I'm "not holding up my end of the bargain"?

I can't undo the past, but I need to fix the present. With Dad gone, we're all we've got, Mom and me. Surely she can see that.

And if she doesn't? Well, I guess I need to show her.

DEE-DUB LACKS SOCIAL GRACES

I invite Dee-Dub to my house after school on Friday. He pulls up at five o'clock and gets out of the car with both of his parents. They shadow him as he walks up the short path, like they're afraid he might get lost.

Mom hovers at the front door, eager to welcome my mysterious new friend. Apart from Alyssa, my only visitors over the past month have been Justin and Carlos. They stopped by when the Little League season was winding down. I guess they figured I'd want to hear about the team. Or maybe they thought I'd be secretly pleased that Logan was in a pitching funk. But they were wrong. I just felt jealous of all of them. When they left after fifteen minutes, I didn't try to stop them. Without baseball, we had nothing to talk about.

I wonder if Dee-Dub and I will find things to talk about now that we're not at school.

Mom answers the door, so she's first to get a full-on look at the Hardesty family. Well, not all of it, because there are two younger siblings acting crazy in the SUV parked outside. But the three people before her are certainly an impressive sight.

"You must be Mrs. Savino," says Mr. Hardesty, shaking her hand. His wife shakes Mom's hand too. Finally, it's Dee-Dub's turn. Looking lost, he pumps Mom's arm up and down hard enough to give her whiplash.

"It's lovely to meet you," Mom says, massaging her hand.

"This is Dee-Dub," says Mrs. Hardesty, beaming.

"Dee-Dub?" says Mom.

Oops. I probably should've warned Mom about this. She may be a little confused.

"It's short for Double-Wide," explains Mr. Hardesty. "That's what his friends call him because he's so big."

Mom's face is frozen in a horrified smile. Dee-Dub's parents don't seem to notice, though, and smile right back, as if comparing a child to a mobile home is the most natural thing in the world.

"You never told me your house is on Hall of Fame Place, Noah," says Dee-Dub.

Mom makes space for me alongside her.

"It's just a block of Elizabeth Avenue," I point out.

"Not just *any* block," says Mr. Hardesty in a scolding tone. "Yogi Berra grew up on this street, and Joe Garagiola." He puffs out his cheeks so that his head resembles an over-inflated soccer ball. "Two Hall of Famers from a single city block. It's remarkable."

Yeah, *remarkable.* And I'm reminded of it every time a bunch of tourists comes along to take pictures and every time I wheel myself over the shiny black plaques in the sidewalk—memorials to those talented boys whose legs worked so much better than mine.

"Bet you're a Cardinals fan, aren't you?" Mr. Hardesty continues.

Seeing Dee-Dub's dad makes me think of my own father and all the times we went to Busch Stadium. Am I still a fan if I never go to a game again?

"It's hard to live in St. Louis and *not* support the Cardinals," Mom says, filling the silence.

"We're already discovering that," says Mrs. Hardesty, laughing. She places her hand on Dee-Dub's shoulder and gives a squeeze. "We'll let you boys get on, then. When should we come back?"

"How about a couple hours?" says Mom. "I've got pizzas for dinner."

"Wonderful!" Mrs. Hardesty spins around as an ear-splitting shriek comes from the SUV. "Kids!" she says.

Dee-Dub waves to his parents as they leave. It'd be kind of sweet if he weren't the size of an average high school senior.

"I'm taking Flub out for a walk," Mom tells me. "You'll be all right, won't you?"

She never usually asks me that. It's almost like she's looking for permission to go.

"We're fine," I say. "I'm not sure that Flub is, though."

Flub belches in agreement.

As Mom drags our elderly dog outside, I lead Dee-Dub into the living room. When he catches sight of the computer monitor, he rushes forward.

"You play Minecraft!" he exclaims. He grabs Mom's office chair and wheels it in front of the screen. Placing one hand on the keyboard and the other on the mouse, he begins to explore my city at warp speed.

"Nice," he murmurs, checking out the skyscrapers. "Cool river too."

"Thanks," I say. "It's called the Mississippi. It's, like, five miles away."

He comes to a dead stop and points at the screen. "What's that?"

"It's the Gateway Arch."

"Really? The proportions are all wrong. Yours is a semicircle." He zooms in and out so quickly I feel motion sick. "The real Gateway Arch is a flattened catenary arch. Plus, the height is precisely the same as the distance between the base of the legs."

In the time it takes me to say "Oh," Dee-Dub obliterates the Gateway Arch. Seriously, in one moment, I have a recognizable replica of St. Louis's most famous monument; in the next, he's zapped the whole thing into outer space.

"W-w-what are you doing?" I ask, but it's too late. Dee-Dub is like a black hole, and my arch has just been swallowed.

Then he begins to rebuild. Not block by careful block, but in waves, as if the new Gateway Arch is being constructed by a gazillion microscopic ants.

"Uh, Dee-Dub?"

"Yeah?"

"How much time do you spend on Minecraft?"

He doesn't take his eyes off the screen, and he doesn't slow down. "As long as I like, once all my homework's done."

"How long does that take?"

"About ten minutes. Sometimes less."

The arch grows upward as fast as Jack's beanstalk. That was made with magic beans, though. What's Dee-Dub's secret?

"You're pretty smart, huh?" I say.

"I like problems that have a clear and quantifiable solution," he replies.

It's lucky we're alone. An answer like that might not go down well at school.

Mom must be standing just outside the house, because I can hear her talking. For a moment, I wonder if she overheard what Dee-Dub just said and found it funny. But then I hear Mr. Dillon's voice too.

So *that's* why she wanted to take Flub out—so she could spend more quality time with her new best friend. And from the sound of it, he's coming inside with her right now.

I wheel backward and slam the living-room door shut. I may not be able to keep Mr. Dillon out of our house, but I can at least put a door between us.

"Are you all right?" Dee-Dub asks without looking at me. "You got quiet."

When Angelica told me to share my *feelings* with someone, I'm not sure she had Dee-Dub in mind. He probably isn't even listening. Maybe that's what makes it easier to open up to him.

"It's my mom," I say as laughter fills the hallway. "She's made friends with this guy down the street, and I don't like him."

"Ah," says Dee-Dub, nodding. "Does his dog pee in your yard?"

"Huh? No. I don't think he's got a dog."

"Does he double-park his car?"

"How would I know?"

Dee-Dub puffs out his cheeks. "No offense, Noah, but it sounds like you don't know him at all."

"I do! His name is Odell Dillon. He works at Busch Stadium. His wife left him last year. And now he keeps hanging out with my mom, and I'm sick of it!"

I shut up quickly. If I'm not careful, Mom will hear me.

Dee-Dub doesn't say anything, but he leaves Minecraft and opens a new browser window. Then he enters all the information I just told him about Mr. Dillon. A moment later, he's zipping through pages of results. "Odell Dillon," he says, scanning a page. "Elizabeth Avenue. Thirty-eight years old. Refuse consultant."

It takes me a moment to translate "refuse consultant" into plain English. I think it means trash collector.

"What do you want to know about him?" Dee-Dub asks.

I'm not sure how to answer that. I suppose what I'd really like is some dirt on Mr. Dillon that means it's okay for me to hate him. I bet that Dee-Dub could find some too—his specialty is problems with a clear and quantifiable solution. But a part of me feels bad for Mr. Dillon now. It's not like anyone grows up dreaming about collecting trash for a living.

Dee-Dub must be tired of waiting, because he returns to Minecraft and begins work on the decorative lake beside the arch. It clearly doesn't meet his standards of aquatic perfection. I could point out that it's *my* lake and *my* city, but it's not like I own St. Louis. If he can make it more perfect, I should probably let him.

"I've been thinking about Wednesday's pitch-off," he says, eyes fixed on the screen. "About how you caught Logan's pitches every time. It was extremely impressive."

"Thanks," I say. "I used to practice a lot before my accident. My dad and I would go to Berra Park, and he'd throw balls to me."

Dee-Dub puffs out his cheeks. "He must've been an amazing pitcher."

"Terrible, actually. That's why I got good at catching. I never knew where the ball was going to go." I let out a little laugh. "Come to think of it, neither did he. Which is kind of amazing considering how many Cardinals games we went to."

I expect Dee-Dub to smile, but he seems deep in thought. When he returns his attention to the monitor, I can guess what's coming. "Where *is* your dad, Noah?"

"I'd rather not talk about that right now."

"Okay." Step by step, he improves my world. "But where is he?"

"Geez, Dee-Dub! He's dead, okay?"

How will he respond? Will it be . . .

(1) Shocked silence followed by an apology, like he's responsible?

(2) A heartfelt quotation from the bible (or one of those poems that uses really long, old-fashioned words)?

(3) Sudden, sympathetic weeping? (This is my least favorite.)

Dee-Dub takes a deep breath and nods. "So, how'd he die?"

Seriously? Trust Dee-Dub to create a number four.

"Like I said, I really don't want to talk about it."

"Gotcha." He finishes the lake, which glistens under the light of an artificial sun, and begins to level the uneven ground on the other side of the Gateway Arch. "Was it cancer?"

I sigh. "No. It wasn't cancer."

"A bowel infection?"

"Uh . . ."

"Cholera?"

"What's cholera?"

"This really nasty disease they have in third-world countries where there's no sanitation. I read about it."

"Why would my dad die of that?"

He grunts. "No idea. But I was running out of natural causes."

"Car accident!" I snap. "He died in a freaking car accident."

"Oh," says Dee-Dub. "You must miss him a lot."

"Yeah."

Then I wonder: How much is a lot? When I was in the hospital, I thought about my dad all the time. Then I left and I thought about him almost every hour. I still think about him every day but not like I used to. It's like he's slipping away from me all over again. I feel sad when I think of him and guilty when I don't.

Dee-Dub is focused on the game again, so he doesn't notice me wiping tears from my cheeks.

"Do you always ask whatever you want?" I say.

"Yeah. My parents say I'm lacking in social graces."

"What does that mean?"

"I have no idea."

He leans back in the office chair and admires his Minecraft empire. I have to admit, it's a really pretty version of our city. Hard to imagine that anything bad could happen in a city like that.

Which goes to show how unrealistic Minecraft is. And how much more there is to life than the things we can see.

FLY BALL!

Once he's rebuilt every part of the Gateway Arch grounds, Dee-Dub starts recreating the Mississippi River. That's when the doorbell rings.

"Have I been here two hours?" he asks me.

"No." I wonder if it's Makayla come looking for her dad. "Come on. I need your help to get rid of someone."

He follows me out of the living room and along the hallway. He even stands beside me as I wrestle open the front door, which must make us seem like a pretty forceful pair—almost like those guys in the X-Men movies: Xavier and Magneto. Well, except that I'm no genius, and the only metal that Dee-Dub bends is the stuff on Minecraft. Not that it matters, anyway, because our guest isn't Makayla.

"Hi, Dee-Dub," says Alyssa brightly. She has a baseball bat slung over her shoulder. "I didn't know you were here too."

Dee-Dub looks uncertainly from Alyssa to me and back again. "I'm here to help get rid of you."

Alyssa frowns. "What?"

"No," I say, frantically waving my hands. "Dee-Dub's got it all wrong. I thought you were someone else."

"Do you often try to get rid of visitors?" she asks calmly.

"It's complicated."

"No kidding." She puffs out her cheeks. "So, are you ready for our practice?"

"Shoot. I totally forgot!"

"What practice?" asks Dee-Dub, who probably wants to keep practicing Minecraft.

"Logan wanted a pitching rematch," Alyssa explains. "Noah said yes."

Dee-Dub scrunches up his face. "I don't know, Noah. I'm not sure you'll be able to pitch as well as Logan."

"I'm catching," I say.

"And I'm pitching," says Alyssa, with a wave of her hand.

"Oh. Then we definitely need to practice," says Dee-Dub,

strolling through the door. The Mississippi River will have to wait a while longer for its makeover, I guess.

Alyssa steps aside to let him pass. "You still okay with this?" she asks me gently.

"Yeah. I think so."

I wheel myself along the hallway and grab my mask and Dad's old-fashioned catcher's mitt from the basket at the bottom of the kitchen cupboard. I put the mitt there after Dad died because I couldn't stand to look at it anymore, and it wasn't like I had any use for it. Not until today, anyway. It feels strange to hold it again, with its familiar scent and soft brown leather all scuffed from years of playing catch together.

There are three steps leading from our porch to the path. That might not sound like much, but it may as well be Mount Everest when you're in a wheelchair. Even the temporary wooden ramp built off to the side is a little steep, so I have to take it real slow. If I lose control, I'll face-plant onto concrete.

Alyssa waits for me. "I like Dee-Dub," she says as he ambles along the street twenty yards ahead of us. "He's, uh, quirky."

"You can say that again."

"Kind of strange that he didn't start school until now, though, right?"

"I guess. I haven't asked him about it."

Across the street, old Mr. Riggieri is sitting in his rocker on the front porch. "You kids playing baseball?" he calls out.

"Seems like it!" I shout back.

"You don't look like any team I've ever seen." He sucks on the inside of his mouth. "This should be good."

"Ignore him," says Alyssa as we slide between parked cars. "He has no idea what's coming."

He's not the only one. Last time Alyssa pitched, she hobbled the mighty Logan Montgomery. Dee-Dub's parents won't be happy if she performs the same trick on their son.

Alyssa hands Dee-Dub the bat, and he and I head down the street a few more yards.

"Okay, here's the deal," I tell him. "Today, you're just here to give us a strike zone. Don't swing at the ball."

"Affirmative," he says. "About that . . . Does Alyssa realize there are cars parked on either side of the street?"

"Hey! My aim isn't *that* bad," she says.

Dee-Dub looks at me. I look at Dee-Dub. I'm not sure we agree with her.

Once we're ready, Alyssa pulls a ball from her shorts pocket and rubs it between her hands. Then she nods at me like I've just given her a signal and corkscrews her body—left leg cocked, right arm pulled back. In a flash, she unwinds.

94

The ball hisses though the air and comes to a dead stop in Dee-Dub's gut.

"Gnffff!" He drops the bat and doubles over. "Gnnnn!"

Mr. Riggieri erupts in laughter.

"Oh, my gosh! I'm so sorry!" cries Alyssa. She chases the ball down before it rolls under a car. "Are you okay?"

Dee-Dub peers up at her. "Ow," he says.

"The pitch totally got away from me!" She stares at the ball accusingly. "The velocity was good, though, right?"

"Not for Dee-Dub it wasn't," I say.

She purses her lips. "Let's do it again."

Dee-Dub looks scared. "Do I have to?" he whimpers.

"She'll make adjustments," I assure him. "It's what pitchers do."

I slide my glove down and away a couple inches. We're working the corner of the strike zone here, which should reduce the chance of her whacking Dee-Dub again.

Alyssa winds up and unleashes another fastball. This one stays down. Down, down, down, and in, where it makes contact with the edge of Dee-Dub's sneaker.

"Daaaa!" He hops up and down. "My ffffffffff!"

Mr. Riggieri is laughing hysterically and smacking his thigh like a crazy man, which isn't very nice.

"Oh, geez! Sorry!" shouts Alyssa. "But I was closer that time, right?"

"Closer to *what*?" I ask.

She retrieves the ball as Dee-Dub bites back the pain. What are his parents going to say when they come to pick him up? He looks like a boxer who's already been knocked down twice and can't decide whether to keep fighting or stay down for the count.

When he finally stands, there's something different about him. He seems tense, like a coiled spring. If I didn't know better, I'd say he wants to pulverize the ball.

"Focus on the middle of the zone," I tell Alyssa. "Go for location, not speed."

She gives a brisk nod and winds up. This time the ball heads straight for my glove. It's a perfect pitch. Absolutely freaking perfect.

At least until Dee-Dub swings the bat.

It happens in an instant: a swing so powerful that the bat tip slices the air like a whip. There's a loud crack, and instead of holding the ball in my mitt, I'm watching it sail upward, upward, upward.

For a couple seconds, I wonder if I've ever seen a ball hit so hard or fly so high. Then it stops rising, crests, and begins to fall. And my thoughts shift to the even bigger question of where it will land.

Alyssa dances around, hands up, trying to put herself in position to make the catch. She isn't wearing a glove, but I don't think she cares. She's willing to take one for the team because the alternative could be catastrophic.

The ball picks up speed as it drops. "I've got it!" Alyssa shouts as if there are other fielders fighting her for the chance to make the catch. "I've got it!"

Except she hasn't got it. She collides with Mr. Riggieri's Buick and topples over. A half second later, the ball collides with the same car.

The windshield, to be precise.

The sound of shattering glass only lasts a moment, but that's plenty long enough for Mr. Riggieri to stop laughing.

Heaving herself off the ground, Alyssa stares at me. "I'm sorry," she says, her voice shaking. "It's all my fault. Do you know whose car this is?"

Oh, yes. I know whose car it is, all right. He's sitting on his porch, sucking the inside of his mouth thoughtfully.

"Sorry, Mr. Riggieri!" I yell. "It was an accident."

Dee-Dub shakes his head. "Not really. I meant to hit the ball."

Alyssa glares at him. "But you didn't mean to hit the car!"

"That's true," says Dee-Dub. "But I wasn't really thinking about the whole landing issue."

Mr. Riggieri steps down from his porch gingerly and approaches his car. I'm not sure why. A smashed-in window looks the same from any angle.

I wheel over to him. "We'll pay for the damage," I say.

"It's not a cheap fix," he replies sternly. He rubs his cheeks, the skin as worn as old leather. "I'm not sure I understand why you're playing baseball on a residential street in the first place. What if you'd hit a kid? Or an old person?"

"Old like you?" says Dee-Dub.

I don't think Dee-Dub is helping our cause.

"We'll do whatever we can to make things right," says Alyssa. "Like Noah says, we'll pay for the windshield."

Mr. Riggieri shakes his head. "I don't want your money. I've got insurance for that. I have a better idea. Meet me at Berra Park tomorrow morning. Ten o'clock. The next few Saturdays, you're going to do some cleaning up." He turns away and traipses back to his porch. "Oh, and don't be late," he adds, "or I'll track you all down and murder you in your sleep."

"Really?" says Dee-Dub.

Mr. Riggieri sighs. "No, son. Not really. But you still better be there. I think you owe me that much."

I AM A HUMAN TRASH CAN

Alyssa and Dee-Dub are already waiting for me when I finish wheeling the quarter mile to Berra Park on Saturday morning. The park is an open space the size of a couple football fields. Everyone thinks it's named for local Hall-of-Famer Yogi Berra, but it's not. There was a politician on The Hill named Berra too—no relation. I guess Berra was a popular name back then.

There's a playground at the edge of the park. I used to come here all the time when I was a little kid. There's a shelter too, and the neighborhood holds parties on national holidays. I haven't been to one since the accident.

Mr. Riggieri shows up a couple minutes after me. He's carrying a roll of black trash bags in one hand and three pairs of work gloves in the other.

"Thanks for doing this," he says, handing out the gloves to us. "It's nice of you."

"Uh . . . sure," Alyssa replies. "It's nice of you not to make us pay for the windshield."

"*Really* nice," I agree.

"And it was nice of you not to tell my parents," adds Dee-Dub. "Yesterday was the first time they let me go out since we got to St. Louis."

Mr. Riggieri peels off a few trash bags. "If you don't mind me asking, what exactly were you three trying to do yesterday?"

"We were practicing," I say. "There's this contest. Alyssa needs to beat the school's best pitcher in a one-on-one duel."

Mr. Riggieri sucks in his cheeks. "No offense," he tells her, "but from what I saw, it looks like your plan is to bludgeon him to death."

"Not really," says Alyssa. "I already did that once. This time I want to win fair."

"And who's coaching you?"

"I am," I say.

"Oh, dear Lord." Mr. Riggieri sighs deeply. "You three get on with cleaning up. I'll be back in ten minutes."

A moment later, we each have a trash bag, and Mr. Riggieri is leaving the park.

"Well, that's strange," says Alyssa. She whips a black trash bag through the air to open it. "Hold this," she tells me.

I take the bag from her. "I feel like a mobile trash can."

"Pretty much," she agrees. "I'm going to fill it with Dee-Dub."

"I don't think Dee-Dub's going to fit."

She rolls her eyes. "Ha-ha."

We start by picking up trash beside the bronze statue of Louis G. "Midge" Berra. Then we move to the bouncy red surface of the playground. Dee-Dub has trouble getting under the slide and climbing equipment, so Alyssa takes care of those.

When we're finished with the playground, we move on to the field. There's a baseball diamond in one corner, and several empty energy-drink bottles have been tossed against the protective chain-link fence behind home plate. Alyssa picks one up and throws it toward me from five yards away. Amazingly, it lands in my partially open trash bag.

"Bet you can't do that again," I say.

She cocks an eyebrow. "Oh, yeah?" Bending down, she selects a half-full bottle of yellow energy drink. Then, without any buildup, she lobs it through the air. It flies several yards and lands smack-dab in the middle of my bag.

She picks up another bottle and throws it. *Bam!* Straight in the bag. And another. *Bam!* Straight in the bag. And another, and another.

Three minutes later, all the trash is in the bag, and she missed only once. I mean, are you *kidding* me?

As I watch each object hit its mark, I come to some important conclusions about Alyssa, in the following order:

(1) She has incredible aim.

(2) She has ice in her veins.

(3) Given 1 and 2, she must've known what she was doing when she kneecapped Logan Montgomery three days ago.

Does that mean she deliberately hit Dee-Dub too?

Before I can ask her about this, Mr. Riggieri walks onto the baseball diamond. He has a bat slung over one shoulder and a duffel bag on the other. He takes awkward, heavy strides that kick up clouds of red clay dust.

"You kids work quickly," he says. "Seems like you're already done for today. Only . . ." He lets the duffel bag slide onto the ground and begins to thwack the bat against his open hand. "I'd like to make sure yesterday's accident never happens again."

I gulp. I sure hope he's not about to use that bat on us.

Dee-Dub must be thinking the same thing because he shrinks back. "I promise I won't break your windshield again, sir," he says. "Actually, after yesterday I don't think I'll ever touch a bat again."

"Nonsense," says Mr. Riggieri gruffly. "You've got a nice easy swing. Power to spare. The key is to choose your pitches wisely. And for the pitcher to stop nailing you. So, let's get practicing."

Alyssa and I exchange glances. Is he really coaching us less than twenty-four hours after we put his car in the shop?

"You want to beat your nemesis or not?" grumbles Mr. Riggieri.

"Absolutely," says Alyssa.

"Then, come on!"

He tosses her a ball, hands me a mitt and mask, and holds out a helmet for Dee-Dub. While Dee-Dub attempts to stuff the helmet on his head, Alyssa sets about kneading the ball between her fingers, the way pro baseball pitchers do.

With the helmet squished tight around his noggin,

Dee-Dub shoots me a desperate look. It's the expression of someone who is smart enough to realize that pitchers do not perfect their craft overnight, and he doesn't want any more bruises to prove it.

"Here," coaxes Mr. Riggieri, trying to hand him the bat. "You're going to be okay, son."

Dee-Dub clearly disagrees, and Dee-Dub is the smartest kid I know. But he still takes the bat with trembling hands and slopes away to home plate. I wheel along beside him. When we're in position, I slide on the mask and glove and wait for Alyssa's first wild pitch.

Sure enough, she winds up and unleashes a doozy: a slider that keeps its path right up to the moment that it curves inward and has a nibble at Dee-Dub's impressive belly.

"Yeoooooow!" howls Dee-Dub.

"Whoa!" Mr. Riggieri is laughing like a maniac. "Dang it, girl. You keep doing that, you better learn to fight. That's how dugout-clearing brawls get started."

"Sorry, Dee-Dub," says Alyssa.

Dee-Dub raises a hand. I think it's his way of saying *I forgive you,* but it also looks like he's trying to surrender.

"If you don't mind me asking," says Mr. Riggieri, still

focused on Alyssa instead of her victim, "what exactly are you aiming for?"

Alyssa bites her lip. "I'm aiming for the strike zone. You know, the area where Dee-Dub is supposed to be able to hit the ball."

"Oh, I know what a strike zone is, all right. I'm just surprised that you do, seeing as how you keep roughing up your friend here." Mr. Riggieri indicates Dee-Dub, who at this moment is cowering behind me. "Just now, when I got back here, I saw you tossing trash into a bag. Do you know why you can do that but you can't nail your pitches?"

Alyssa shakes her head.

"You don't aim for a *zone*. You aim for a target. And in baseball, your target is Noah's glove. Lock in on that glove, and let the ball fly."

"Oh." Alyssa fingers the end of her braid. "That actually makes sense."

Mr. Riggieri raises an eyebrow. "I'm glad you think so."

With a deep breath, Alyssa prepares to throw another pitch. I position my glove in the middle of the strike zone, and she nods. Then she winds up, throws the ball, and—

Crack. Dee-Dub hits that sucker so hard he breaks the

wooden bat in two. The ball climbs up and up, and keeps on going until it lands in the far outfield.

Laughter ripples over from the playground. It's Logan Montgomery, taking in the action from an elevated platform meant for little kids. "That was awesome!" he yells. "You pitch like that, Choo, you're going to make me look even more amazing than I already am!"

Alyssa closes her eyes, fuming. Mr. Riggieri gives Logan an icy stare. Even Dee-Dub seems to be regretting the hit, and not just because he destroyed a bat.

I couldn't care less about Logan, though, because I just saw two incredible things. (1) Alyssa made a pitch that flew as fast and straight as a laser beam, and (2) Dee-Dub hit it only because he sneaked a peek at my glove before she let it go. From that, just as in math, he must have calculated the flight of the ball and the point of impact. And he launched the ball so far, I'm surprised it didn't carry on clear across Missouri.

Logan's still laughing, but I think I see a way to wipe that smile off his face for good. If Alyssa keeps her pitches on target, she's got a heck of a fastball. And if Dee-Dub bats instead of her, anything is possible—especially if he knows which pitch Logan's about to make. And I can make sure he knows too because I'm the catcher. I call the pitches.

I may not be able to play Little League anymore, but taking down Wellspring Middle School's home-run king with Alyssa and Dee-Dub . . .

Well, that might just be the next best thing.

SPELL CHECKER

When I get home, Mom and Mr. Dillon are side by side at the kitchen sink, Mom's washing the dishes and Mr. Dillon is drying them. I hate how comfortable he looks, like he thinks he belongs here.

I guess it's not so surprising, though. A week ago, he helped her unload grocery bags. Since then, she's spent as much time with him as she has with me.

Makayla is sitting at the kitchen table, brows furrowed. She looks as annoyed at our parents as I am. Then her expression brightens, and she says, "Serendipity. S-E-R-E-N-D-I-P-I-T-Y. Serendipity."

"Yes!" cries Mom, spinning around. "That's amazing." She turns to me. "Makayla's studying for the spelling bee, honey."

"Already?" I say. "Isn't that in January?"

Makayla nods. "The school one is, yeah. But we're doing a practice bee in class this week."

I roll up to the kitchen table and study the vocabulary sheet. Some of these words are crazy hard. I pick the worst of all. "Spell 'Sisyphean.'"

She puckers up her lips. "Can you give me a definition?"

Rats! I forgot about this part of the bee. "Um, it's a, uh . . . an impossible task. Or is it a pointless task?" I wave the thought away. "It's one or the other."

"Can you use it in a sentence?"

"Spelling bees are Sisyphean."

Mom narrows her eyes at me but doesn't say anything.

Makayla straightens in her chair. Puts on her game face. "Sisyphean. S-I-S-I-P-H-E-A-N. Sisyphean."

"Naaaa!" I make a sound like a demented bee. "I'm afraid that's incorrect."

"It was close," insists Mom.

I nod gravely. "If only they gave points for effort."

"Well, maybe they should! Effort counts for a lot. I think

110

it's very admirable that Makayla's spending her weekend trying to get better."

I don't think this is about Makayla anymore. Or spelling
bees. I think it's about me and physical therapy.

"I'd be spending my weekend *getting better* too," I say,
"except I was busy picking up trash at Berra Park."

"That's great, Noah," replies Mr. Dillon, eager to show his
support. "What inspired you to do that?"

"He didn't have any choice," snaps Mom. "He was playing
baseball in the middle of the street last night. . . . Broke Mr.
Riggieri's windshield."

"*You* did that?" asks Mr. Dillon.

"Do I look like I can use a baseball bat?" I deadpan.

Mom shoots me an angry look. Mr. Dillon backs off too. I
think he's reconsidering his place on Team Noah.

For several moments, we're all silent. Then Mr. Dillon
folds the tea towel he's been using and hangs it on the oven
door. "Well, it sounds like you've had a busy morning, son."

My entire body goes rigid. I am a lot of things, but I am
not his son.

"I'll bet you're hungry as heck," he continues. "Hot salami
sub from Gioia's sound good?"

Of course it sounds good. I've eaten enough of Gioia's hot salami to feed my entire school for a week. But I want to grab a sandwich with Mr. Dillon about as much as I want to share the school elevator with Flub and his leaky butt.

"I'm not hungry," I say.

"Fair enough," says Mr. Dillon amiably. "What about cannoli from Missouri Baking, then?"

"No thanks."

"Noah," says Mom in a warning tone.

"I'm just not hungry," I lie.

She touches my forehead like she's checking for a fever. "You feeling all right?"

I jerk my head away. "It was the dog, not me."

Nobody laughs. Flub isn't even in the room with us. I've ruined the atmosphere now. Mom and Mr. Dillon and Makayla were getting along great until I showed up. Mom was flipping out over Makayla's mental database of exceedingly long and useless words. But she's not so impressed with me.

"Fine," says Mom curtly. "We'll see you later, then. Shall I ask Kathy to check in on you?"

It's a cheap shot, but maybe I deserve it. "I'll survive without her," I say. "And you."

Mom flinches. I didn't mean that last part. I'm angry with Mr. Dillon, not her. But these days Mom seems to be on his side more than mine.

As Mom circles the kitchen table, Makayla points to the spelling bee sheets. "Should I take these with me? They're my only copies."

"Leave them here," says her dad.

"They'll be perfectly safe," agrees Mom.

Makayla does as she's told, but as she follows the adults out of the kitchen, she lingers a moment, her eyes shifting between the pages and me. She's giving me a warning look that says, *Feed these pages to Flub and I will DESTROY you.*

I know better than to underestimate Little Miss Perfect after her quaking-face routine the other night, but right now I'd do anything to shut her up. So I return a defiant look that says, *Game on, little girl. Game on!*

Then I sit in the kitchen, alone and hungry, and try to think of a way to balance the scales.

It doesn't take me long to come up with a plan.

And for once, it's pure genius.

I saw this old James Bond movie once. The criminal mastermind was named Blofeld. He used a wheelchair, and wore a monocle, and talked in a menacing foreign accent, and spent all day stroking his white cat. I don't have a monocle, a cat, or a foreign accent, but I've got the wheelchair, and I'm just as evil as he was.

Don't believe me?

Just watch as I open up a new document on my computer. See me match the font and point size to the words on Makayla's sheet. Then marvel as I copy every single word on her sheet, only with a few minor changes.

I am like the anti–spell check. I can take perfectly composed words and ruin them. I can crush consonants and violate vowels. I am the grim reaper of the spelling bee, and I will show no mercy.

Makayla, my chirpy little friend, you and your unwelcome father had this coming.

RUNNING ISN'T EPIC

Monday, September 18, aka my birthday. Unfortunately, it's also a B day on the Wellspring Middle School schedule, and since Congress hasn't gotten around to declaring my birthday a national holiday yet, I'm stuck in PE.

My classmates are warming up by running around the gym ten times. Mrs. Friendly has even placed cones at strategic points so that no one can cut the corners.

She's nice like that.

Logan is hobbling along near the back while his super-fit teammates stride out half a lap ahead of him.

Mrs. Friendly is not impressed. "Pick it up, Montgomery," she barks. "You ought to be running a sub-seven-minute mile in seventh grade. The way you're going, you'll be lucky to finish in a day!"

Logan glares at Mrs. Friendly. Then Alyssa laps him, and he glares at her too. Finally, he catches me smiling and throws me a gut-churning death stare as well.

Unfortunately, Mrs. Friendly notices Logan's death stare, which is how she discovers my hiding place behind the bleacher seats.

"And what do you think *you're* doing, Savino?" she growls.

I wheel forward as if I've only just arrived in PE, but Mrs. Friendly isn't fooled. I've tried this trick before, and anyway, the entrance is at the other end of the gym.

She stands as rigid as a column, hands on her hips and lips pursed like she's considering my punishment. She must have a lot of punishments in mind, because she doesn't say anything for a long time. Will it be fifty laps of the gym? Detention? A fistfight with one of those endangered polar bears from Makayla's Gabriella Masterson books?

With a sigh, Mrs. Friendly walks over to me and takes a seat on the bleachers. "So, it's your birthday, huh?" she says.

"Uh . . ." I can't believe she knows that. I've tried to keep it under wraps.

"I was looking up fitness guidelines for a boy in a wheelchair," she explains. "I needed to know your age, so I checked your date of birth. If you're twelve today, you must've skipped a grade."

"I went straight from pre-K to first grade. My mom says I was tall back then and good at math. I guess I peaked too soon."

Smiling, Mrs. Friendly gives my shoulder a gentle punch. I pretend it doesn't hurt. "Well, happy birthday," she says.

"Um, thanks."

She jumps up suddenly. "I said pick it up, Montgomery!"

Logan waits for her to look away and shakes his head in disgust.

"So," she says, "I saw you catching for Alyssa and Logan at their little pitch-off last week. It clearly wasn't your first rodeo, so I asked Logan about it. He said you used to play Little League."

"Not anymore," I say.

"What do you do instead?"

"I push myself around in a wheelchair."

117

She flexes her biceps, or triceps, or whatever those upper arm muscles are that make her look like she could take down a mountain lion. "I mean, what other talents have you been hiding?"

"Oh. Well, I can count to ten in Spanish."

"That's not exactly what I mean."

"I know the capital of Missouri is Jefferson City."

"Or that."

Mrs. Friendly looks menacingly at my classmates, who pick up the pace immediately.

"Do you know why I do CrossFit competitions, Noah?" she asks, sitting again.

"Because they pay you?

"No."

"Because you get on TV?"

"No."

"Hmm. Then I honestly can't think of a single reason."

She leans forward, her fingers knitted together. "I do it because I know that nothing is forever. You hear me?"

I can't believe she just said that. If there's anyone in the school who's learned that lesson, it's me.

"Even if I'm lucky enough to live a long and healthy life," she continues, "there will come a time when my body says,

Enough. Little by little, I'll slow down. My muscles will weaken. I won't be able to do the things I used to do."

She stares off into the distance as if she's seeing beyond the gym to a future without PE. I follow her gaze and imagine that future too. It looks pretty awesome, to be honest.

"*That* is why I work out like crazy, Noah." She stabs the air with her finger. "So that I can put off that day. And when it finally comes, I'll be so fit, I'll still be better off than most of the people around me." She nods to herself. "I'll also know that I've pushed myself to the limit—seen what this old body of mine can do. You understand what I'm saying?"

"I think so," I say, which is my usual response when either (1) I haven't been listening, or (2) I don't have a clue what an adult is talking about.

This time I actually mean it, though: I *do* understand, because it's the same thing Angelica has been telling me for months. But if hard work is everything, why is Dee-Dub still lagging behind One-Leg Logan?

Or is he? Digging deep for an extra gear, Dee-Dub slowly closes the gap. It's kind of epic, like the climax to a movie. I can almost hear the crowd cheering him on. I imagine him surging ahead, stealing victory at the finish line.

Is this what victory would look like for me? Lumbering,

awkward, but just as epic. If I work my butt off, maybe the insurance people will get off Mom's back and she could stop stressing out. Maybe we'd get along better again. Maybe she wouldn't want to hang out with Mr. Dillon as much.

Mrs. Friendly slides off the bleacher seat and stands in front of me. "So . . . any thoughts about what I just said?"

I have lots of thoughts, actually. But I'm too busy watching Dee-Dub to share them. He's only a couple yards back from Logan now and closing. I lean forward in my chair, willing him on. I want him to win. I want my epic movie to have a happy ending.

She taps her foot. "Noah?"

Logan must hear Dee-Dub's footsteps, because he looks over his shoulder and sees my slow-charging friend. Immediately, he picks up speed, and the race, if it ever was a race, is over.

My shoulders slump. So much for a happy ending.

"I really want to know what you're thinking," says Mrs. Friendly.

I huff. "I'm thinking that all this stuff about your body breaking down sure does make old age sound like a lot of fun!"

I wonder if she'll laugh or at least applaud my wit. Sarcasm has been my friend for the past few months, and until recently, people always used to like it. But not anymore.

"Well, you know what?" says Mrs. Friendly, not sounding very friendly. "You make being young look like no fun at all, Noah Savino. And that's just a shame."

She turns away and raises the whistle to her mouth. Before she blows it, though, she peers at me over her shoulder. "So, when you want to start changing that, you let me know, okay? I'll be here, and I'll help you any way I can."

Stewing in my chair, I study my legs. Mrs. Friendly has no idea what it's like for me. No one does. Everyone keeps spouting inspirational phrases like they'll change my life, but the words feel as empty as the printed poems on all the sympathy cards we got after Dad died. Words won't turn back time. Words can't fix my legs.

Trouble is, it's not just Mrs. Friendly's and Angelica's and Mom's voices I hear gathering against me. I know that Dad would say the same thing if he were here. He'd show me the Cardinals roster and remind me how many of those players had to overcome injury and rehab stints in the minor leagues. He'd ask me what would've happened to any of them if they'd quit before making it back to the top. Then he'd tell me to get to work.

But if Dad were still here, I wouldn't need to work. Every-thing would be different.

I ball my hands in my lap and watch the last of the runners approach the finish line. Dee-Dub has fallen to the very back. Soon enough, he's the only person still running, huffing and puffing like the Little Engine That Could.

Why did he try to catch Logan? He's a math genius, not a runner. Why not face reality?

He's a mystery to me, Dee-Dub. But of all the things I don't understand, this one ranks at the top: What makes him work so hard when the race is already lost?

ANNUAL CHECKUP

Two things happen after school on my birthday every year:

(1) Dinner at Anthonino's Taverna.

(2) Annual well-child checkup.

The good news is that my checkup means putting off PT until tomorrow. The bad news is that the checkup comes before dinner.

My pediatrician's name is Dr. Marietta Grafton, which makes her sound like a character in one of those stuffy historical dramas that Mom likes to watch on TV on Sunday evenings. Dr. Grafton runs ultra marathons and collects tattoos, though, so I guess they won't be casting her anytime soon.

Once the nurse has finished measuring me, I wait for the doctor. But the young guy who bursts into the room like the star of a Hollywood sitcom is definitely not Dr. Grafton.

"You must be Noah," he says.

"Yeah." (I hope my role in the sitcom is to look confused.)

"Well, thank goodness! Be kind of awkward if I was in the wrong room, wouldn't it?"

"Uh . . ." (On second thought, maybe I've been cast to deliver monosyllabic answers.)

"Where's Dr. Grafton?" Mom asks.

"Slipped when she was out running. Broke her arm in five places. By the time the surgeons are done with her, she'll be carrying more hardware than a Home Depot employee." He shakes his head. "Isn't that the *worst*?"

Neither Mom nor I answer that question.

"I'm Dr. Ferrell, by the way," he continues. "Double-R, E, double-L. Not feral like a cat."

"That's comforting," I say.

Dr. Ferrell cackles. Maybe I'm getting the hang of this sitcom after all.

"So," he says, scanning my file, "seems like you had an accident earlier this year. How are you coping?"

"Fine." (Another one-word answer. I've really got to improve my range.) "It's nice to be able to sit down all the time."

It takes him a moment to realize I'm kidding. "Oh, I get it," he says, rolling his eyes. "Very funny." He doesn't laugh, though. "And I see you're going to PT. Bet you love it, huh?"

"Not really."

"I was kidding."

"Oh."

Our sitcom is definitely missing some comedy. It doesn't help that I can feel Mom getting tenser every moment. She brought me here to see Dr. Grafton, not the new guy. Mom likes Dr. Grafton. She *trusts* her. Dr. Ferrell has big trail-running shoes to fill, and he's not impressing Mom in the starring role.

"It's my birthday," I say, filling the awkward silence.

Dr. Ferrell checks my date of birth on his clipboard as if I might be lying. "Why, yes it is. And you chose to spend it with me! Guess you like doctors, huh?"

"Not really."

"Uh . . ."

"It was my idea," says Mom, clearly not wanting to be left out of this riveting conversation. "I always say, when it comes to health, prevention is better than cure."

"It's true," I say. "She always says that. Like, *always.*"

"I couldn't agree more," says Dr. Ferrell. He looks at the clipboard again. "Well, let's see. Weight is still tracking around fifteenth percentile, so that's good. You've grown, though. Height is up to thirtieth percentile."

"Not when I'm in a wheelchair all day," I point out.

"Well, no. That's true. But again, the growth-trend line is good."

"Phew. My growth-trend line has been keeping me up at night recently."

Dr. Ferrell chokes out a single nervous laugh. Our sitcom is officially over, and I'm just making him uncomfortable now. I can tell by the way he glues his eyes to the clipboard.

"I'm sure I don't need to tell you to avoid alcohol, tobacco, and drugs," he says.

"Right," I say.

He puts a check mark in a box and moves down his list. "Is there a gun in your house?"

"No," says Mom quickly. "Definitely not."

"Good." Dr. Ferrell gives her a particularly big check mark

for that answer. "And what about a bike hel—"

He doesn't actually say "helmet," but I know that's what was coming because he's turning bright red. He puts a check mark anyway and slides his finger onto the next question. "Do you always wear a seat belt, Noah?"

The air in the room seems to thin out. I can't meet his eyes.

"Yes," I say. "I always wear a seat belt."

He checks a box. Then he leans forward and lowers his voice, like we're in on some great secret. "And does your mom ever use a cell phone when she's driving?"

I look at Mom. Mom looks at me. She swallows hard. "Uh, no," she says. "No, I don't."

Dr. Ferrell gives a little smirk. "Is that true, Noah?"

"Yes," I say, gripping my armrests. "It's true."

"What about screen time?" he asks, looking at the next box. "Do you have unsupervised access to the internet?"

I tell myself he's just reading from a checklist. Dr. Grafton used to do the same thing. But everything has changed since last year.

"What about a cell phone?" he continues. "I bet you can't live without it."

"Okay," says Mom, standing abruptly. "I think we should wrap things up."

Dr. Ferrell falls silent. His pen hovers above the box. "Is everything all right?"

Mom is already releasing the brakes on my wheelchair. "Noah doesn't have a cell phone," she says.

"Good for him," says Dr. Ferrell, rewarding me with an especially large check mark. "I keep telling parents, cell phones are responsible for—"

"Okay, then!" exclaims Mom. "Same time next year."

"But . . ." Dr. Ferrell looks at his mostly empty checklist. "Would you prefer to reschedule?"

"Sure. Let's do that."

Mom opens the door, and I wheel myself through. As soon as I'm in the hallway, I pick up speed.

Check this out, Mrs. Friendly. I'm flying!

I don't look back to see if Mom is following me. I don't wait at the front desk in case she wants to reschedule. I just want to get away. Now.

If there's one thing I don't need it's a lesson on how dangerous cell phones can be. Believe me, no one knows the dangers as well as I do.

As I press the button to open the main door, the receptionist tells me to have a nice day.

It's my birthday. This ought to be more than a *nice day*. I should be celebrating. There should be presents and streamers and obscene amounts of junk food. And Dad should be here, celebrating right along with me.

But he's not.

And he never will be again.

DESSERT IS OVERRATED

You can't go a block on The Hill without bumping into an Italian restaurant. The fancy ones are kind of famous—Charlie Gitto's, Gian-Tony's, Lorenzo's, Giovanni's—but we'd need a bank loan to eat in one of them. So we go to Anthonino's, which is great and just around the corner.

There's a short line for tables, so Mom and I wait inside the entrance and smile politely at people as they leave. Little kids check out my wheelchair. I try to smile at them too, but it's harder because some of them stare at me like I'm a Martian.

I am not a Martian.

The TVs behind the bar are showing a Cardinals game,

and the good guys are winning. I ought to be happy, but seeing Busch Stadium in the twilight reminds me of the last time I went to a game there. It was just Dad and me, and the game went to extra innings, and he let me stay till the very end, even though it was well past ten o'clock. Mom has never taken me to a game and I'm pretty sure she never will.

"What are you thinking about?" Mom whispers.

I peer up at her, surprised to discover that my eyes are moist. Okay, a little more than moist actually, which is totally embarrassing. "Nothing," I say.

Her eyes droop. She probably thinks I'm blowing her off, but does she really want me to say how much I miss Dad? It just makes her sad, and it never changes anything.

I feel bad, though. Dad was always the one who filled the silence, not Mom. He loved to talk, and we loved to let him. Now he's gone, and all Mom wants to talk about is school and PT and feelings, and I don't want to discuss those. Maybe that's why she likes hanging out with Mr. Dillon. He's a talker too.

Maybe I *should* open up to her. Tell her exactly how I feel. Maybe she wouldn't need Mr. Dillon to hang around if I were easier to talk to. A birthday's as good a time as any to start over.

"Mom," I say quietly. "I—"

"Well, look who's here!" comes a voice from just behind me.

I crane my neck around. Unbelievable! Mr. Dillon is standing in the restaurant doorway, and everyone's favorite precocious speller, Makayla, is with him.

"Odell!" exclaims Mom. Her face lights up. "What are you doing here?"

"Eating," he says. "You?"

"Eating." She steps over to him, and they share an awkward hug. "It's Noah's birthday."

Mr. Dillon slaps a meaty paw on my shoulder. "Well, happy birthday. Want us to sing to you?"

"About as much as I want food poisoning," I reply.

"Ha-ha-ha." Mr. Dillon's belly rocks with laughter. "You're a funny one. Anyone ever tell you that?"

I pretend not to notice that Mom is glaring at me. "Not recently, no."

A hostess in black sidles up to us. "We have a table ready," she says. "Four of you?"

There's an awkward moment as Mom and Mr. Dillon exchange glances, and Mom and I exchange glances, and Mr. Dillon and I exchange glances.

"I, uh . . ." Mom mumbles, waiting for me to make the call.

I keep my lips sealed. No way am I inviting them to join us.

Makayla slides an arm across my shoulders. "That's right," she says brightly. "Four of us."

Then she trots along beside the hostess, leaving the three of us to follow.

Ordering dinner is as challenging as one of Mr. Kostas's complex math equations. I want to spend as little time with Mr. Dillon and Makayla as possible, but I want to be sure I get dessert. Okay, yes, I'm twelve now, but so what? No one ever said that gelato stops tasting good when you're no longer eleven.

Finally, I work it out: to speed things up, I'll skip the appetizers and order my entrée along with the drinks. It's *my* birthday, so everyone else will have to follow my lead.

Before the waitress returns, Mr. Dillon clears his throat. "So, I didn't know it's your birthday, Noah, but it just so happens I've got tickets to a Cardinals game for you and your mom and Makayla. You can bring a friend, too. Best seats in the place. A week from Friday. What do you say?"

Mom nods enthusiastically. "We'd love to go, wouldn't we, honey?"

I can't believe what I'm hearing. Since when does Mom

want to go to a Cardinals game? Is it just because Mr. Dillon is going to be there?

Anyway, how can a refuse consultant at Busch Stadium afford to give away prime seats to a Cardinals game?

"Those tickets must've cost hundreds of dollars," I say.

He brushes the thought aside. "One of the perks of the job."

"I'm still not clear on what your job is," says Mom.

"Dad is Fredbird!" Makayla stage-whispers.

It's lucky we're not already eating or I'd choke on my food. I've seen Fredbird at Cardinals games—dancing around in his white Cardinals shirt, feathery red shorts, yellow tights, and beaked mask—and I don't think Mr. Dillon could fit inside that mascot suit if his life depended on it.

"That's how he got the tickets," Makayla explains. "He'll be Fredbird at the game. He's even coming to my school in costume tomorrow!"

"Shh!" hisses Mr. Dillon, his eyes darting around the neighboring tables. "We've talked about this, Makayla. You can't tell anyone I'm Fredbird."

"But why not?" Makayla pouts.

Mr. Dillon refuses to answer, but I can think of a hundred reasons why not, starting with the fact that it's *obviously not true*. But how would Makayla have come up with the crazy idea in the first place unless her dad told her it was true?

Even Mom looks unsure. She smiles blandly at Makayla but avoids eye contact with Mr. Dillon and me. "It's a very generous offer, Odell," she says finally. "We'd love to go."

Mr. Dillon rewards her with a smile, but his gaze is fixed on Makayla too. He seems annoyed, and for the first time, I actually feel bad for her. If he's been lying to impress his daughter, then *he* should be ashamed. Sure, she's annoying as heck, but Makayla's just a fourth grader. Of course she's going to believe her dad when he says he's Fredbird.

Two minutes later, we order food. Fifteen minutes after that, the entrees arrive, and I know I've chosen well. I have meatballs and spaghetti. Mom has toasted ravioli, which isn't really an entree, but she knows I love it, and today is my birthday, so

I eat half her toasted ravioli, and she has some of my spaghetti. Meanwhile, Mr. Dillon chows down on a bowl of pasta marinara while Makayla picks at a chicken breast. She's eating so slowly that she still has half the dinner left when the rest of us are done.

I really hope this doesn't mean I'll have to wait for dessert.

"You okay, Makayla?" Mom asks.

Staring at her plate, Makayla gives a sorry nod.

"What is it, honey?" asks Mr. Dillon.

Makayla has been perfectly still and silent, which actually makes a nice change. But just as I'm thinking how much I like this version of her, she begins to sniffle.

Then she whimpers.

Then she sobs.

"Honey!" cries Mr. Dillon. "What's up?"

Isn't it obvious? He lied to his daughter about being Fredbird and got upset when she repeated the lie to me. If I were Makayla, I'd be upset too.

"I . . . I . . ." She gasps tiny choking breaths. "I failed the practice spelling bee. I failed so badly, the teacher says I can't be in the school bee anymore."

Uh-oh.

"But . . ." Mr. Dillon reaches across the table and takes her hand. "Are you sure? You worked real hard on that, and you hardly ever made a mistake."

"I know!" she wails. "It was, like, everything I did was wrong. Just *wrong*!"

Other diners are tuning in now, like we're part of some freak show. *Tonight Only—Hysterical Girl and Wheelchair Boy!*

Across the table, Mom looks utterly baffled. Me? I'm not

baffled at all. But I am kind of worried.

Turns out, I should be too, because after Makayla wipes away her tears, she looks right at me like she *knows* it was me that ruined her chances. Maybe she noticed that some of the spelling words looked different after she left our house on Saturday. If she's still got those sheets I printed out, the investigation will begin. What if our clueless parents trace the crime back to me?

I feel caught. More than that, as Makayla begins to cry again, I feel ashamed. Sure, she's really full of herself, but she wanted to do well. She *worked* for it too, like Dee-Dub chasing Logan in gym.

And what did I do? I stole her dream of winning the spelling bee. I tricked her, just like her father lied to her about being Fredbird.

"I'm sure there'll be other chances," I say.

Mom and Mr. Dillon seem surprised that I'm joining in the conversation—impressed too, like it's a sign that I care about Makayla.

I *do* care. But mostly I'm scared to death.

"There won't be," Makayla says through gritted teeth. "I'm out. Done. It's all over."

We pause our conversation as the waitress returns. "I can box that for you, hon," she tells Makayla. "Now, anyone interested in dessert?"

Mom shakes her head. So does Mr. Dillon. It's my turn, but I'm so nervous I feel like I could barf, so I shake my head as well. The sooner this tragic dinner is over, the better.

The waitress turns to Makayla. I wait for my former nemesis to shake her head, beads jiggling back and forth. Her father let her down. *I* let her down. She must want this evening to be over as much as I do.

Instead, Makayla takes a deep, steadying breath and nods. "Gelato, please," she says.

Happy birthday to me!

CUPS OF FLOUR

While we wait for Mr. Kostas to join us in math class the next day, Logan "entertains" us with a play-by-play of his weekend baseball game—how he pitched a perfect game on only one good leg and even hit a home run. I swear nobody does a better job of making Logan sound heroic than Logan.

Lower lip jutting out, Alyssa blows her bangs away from her face. "You look tired, Noah," she says.

"I didn't sleep well," I admit.

"We can see that," says Dee-Dub. "Your hair is positively vertical in places. Kind of like a peacock's butt feathers."

I glare at him.

"Why can't you sleep?" asks Detective Alyssa.

I'm not going to answer that. Alyssa has always had a soft spot for the underdog, and I don't think she'll approve of what I did to Makayla's spelling sheet. Heck, even I'm finding it hard to like me right now. So I pretend I'm busy opening my backpack. Unfortunately, it's on its side, and half of my books tumble onto the floor, out of reach.

She picks them up for me. "Whatever it is, you should get it off your chest."

The word "chest" reminds me of her boobs, which are unfortunately at eye level again.

Dee-Dub clears his throat. "Noah, are you looking at—"

"No," I snap. "I am *not s*taring at Alyssa's boobs!"

The entire classroom falls silent. Dee-Dub opens his eyes super wide. Alyssa looks like she wants to punch my lights out.

Is this karma for me screwing up Makayla's spelling bee? If it is, I need to make things right soon.

I fold my arms on the desk and rest my head. If I pretend to be asleep, maybe everyone will leave me alone. Even better, I might actually fall asleep.

Or not. Mr. Kostas enters the room and tosses his messenger

bag onto the teacher's desk. He pulls out a stack of math work sheets and distributes one to each student. He gives a little extra *oomph* as he slaps one onto Alyssa's desk.

"For you, Ms. Choo," he says with a voice as sweet as artificial syrup. "Cups of flour in a cake."

I look at the first question: *1 cup of flour weighs 4 1/4 oz.; 1 oz = 28 1/3 grams. How many cups should you use in a cake that requires 800 grams of flour?*

In the time it takes me to yawn, Dee-Dub is already writing the answer: *6 2/3 cups.*

I must be imagining things—there's no way anyone could work out the answer that fast—so I blink hard and look at his sheet again.

The numbers are still there.

Usually, I'd be impressed, but today it just annoys me. While I'm struggling to keep my eyes open, Dee-Dub is doing advanced math in his head.

"You're supposed to show your work," I say.

He pencils in another answer. "Takes too long."

I look at my own sheet. I'll need to divide 800 by the multiple of 4 1/4 and 28 1/3, which requires some serious long multiplication. And then division. I could be doing this question for the rest of class.

Dee-Dub scribbles an answer to question three.

"How do you do that?" I grumble.

"Just do," he says.

"Geez. You're like freaking Einstein."

Dee-Dub's head whips around. "Do *not* call me that."

"Shhh!" hisses Mr. Kostas.

I wait for our teacher to look away. "What's wrong with 'Einstein'?" I ask.

Dee-Dub growls. "I said—"

"Shhh!" Mr. Kostas places his palms flat on his desk. "That's your second warning, Ruben."

But Dee-Dub isn't listening. His full attention is fixed on me, and I'm not sure why. "It's what they called me at my old school," he says.

I don't see what that has to do with anything. I mean, these are the same kids who named him after a trailer. Is he really saying he prefers "Double-Wide" to "Einstein"? If anyone compared me to a famous physicist, I'd be thrilled.

I'm not in the mood to argue, though. "Fine," I say. "I won't call you Einstein again."

His eyes open wide. His jaw muscles flex. Somehow, I've made him even angrier.

"Ruben," snaps Mr. Kostas. "If you don't get on with the work sheet right now . . ."

It's like Dee-Dub can't hear him. And he definitely does *not* look like a student who plans to get on with his work sheet. Mr. Kostas must think so too because he pushes back his chair and stands.

Suddenly, I remember the look on Dee-Dub's face when he smacked Alyssa's pitch through Mr. Riggieri's windshield. He'd taken two hits to the body without losing his cool, but then he snapped. He didn't care whether it was sensible to hit the ball. He didn't even seem to notice where he was or what he was doing. He just swung at the pitch with everything he had, like his body was under the control of some invisible force.

Now I think that force is back, and it's about to land him in a whole heap of trouble.

"Mr. Kostas," I say as our teacher strides toward us, "I . . . uh . . ."

I throw Alyssa a desperate look. She raises her hand immediately.

"Excuse me, Mr. Kostas," she calls out.

Our teacher freezes. "Yes?"

"I have a problem."

"Don't tell me: you don't like cake."

"No. It's that this recipe won't actually make a cake. It's missing eggs. And baking powder. And sugar. And butter."

"Oh," says Mr. Kostas.

"Yes," continues Alyssa. "And so I wondered if there was another part. Just to make sure it all makes sense."

Mr. Kostas deflates. "Ms. Choo, I'm not a home economics teacher."

Lips pressed tightly together, Alyssa nods. "I realize that, Mr. Kostas. And you're wonderful, of course, but . . . you're always telling us about the real-world applications of mathematics. This isn't real-world."

"It's just a cake!"

"Not really. Without the egg and baking powder, the batter won't rise. It'll be a powdery mess."

Everyone snickers. Mr. Kostas narrows his eyes. "Do you really want a detention, Ms. Choo?"

"No!" cries Alyssa. She shifts her eyes back and forth between our teacher and Dee-Dub, who is still huffing and puffing like the big bad wolf. "I'm serious. We've been looking at this sheet nonstop for the past five minutes, and it'll *never make a cake.* It's like reading a book in English and pretending the main character doesn't exist. Or memorizing the US states in Social Studies but pretending that Alaska and Hawaii don't count because they're not contiguous. It's like—"

"Enough!" Mr. Kostas waves his hand, but it may as well be a white flag. He returns to his seat and breathes in and out slowly. "Please, *please* . . . just finish the sheet, won't you?"

Alyssa glances at Dee-Dub, who seems to be channeling his anger into completing the math problems even faster than usual. Satisfied that the danger has passed, Alyssa gives our stressed-out teacher a sympathetic nod and buckles down to work again.

I wait a few seconds and peer at her from the corner of my eye. It's just as well she's a quick thinker or the situation could've ended badly. I give her a thumbs-up and wait for her to do the same.

Alyssa manages a smile but only just. And she definitely doesn't give me a thumbs-up. In fact, gnawing the end of her pencil like a starving beaver, she looks right past me to Dee-Dub. From her expression, I'd say that of all the problems she'll be asked to solve today, he might be the one that confuses her most of all.

FREDBIRD HAS SLIMMED DOWN

St. Louis Public Schools uses the same set of buses for elementary, middle, and high schools, so our day begins and ends two hours before the elementary schools. This is absolutely as popular with my classmates as you would imagine, which is probably why most of them sleep through homeroom.

But today, the crazy schedule suits me. I'm still feeling bad about my part in Makayla's spelling bee fiasco, and the way I see it, my only chance to set the record straight without Mom or Makayla finding out is for me to explain everything to her teacher in person. Luckily, Makayla goes to the same elementary school I used to go to. Even luckier, Fredbird is making a special guest appearance this afternoon, which gives me just the excuse I need to be there.

"Mom," I say, buckling into my seat after school. "Can we stop off at my old school? I'd really like to see Mr. Dillon being Fredbird."

"You've got physical therapy," she says.

"At four o'clock."

Mom shuffles in her seat. "Why do you want to see him?"

"Are you kidding? Fredbird's a legend. How many kids get to say they know him personally?"

"You won't say anything of the sort," she replies. "A lot of those kids think Fredbird's real."

"You're saying he's *not*?" I pull a sad face in the rearview mirror and wobble my lower lip. "You just burst my bubble!"

Mom doesn't play along with my lame attempt at humor. Something tells me she's just as suspicious about Mr. Dillon's claim as I am.

"You can have fifteen minutes," she says finally. "But don't you dare embarrass Fredbird."

I'm not sure how you embarrass a mascot, but I keep this

thought to myself. After all, Mom just said "Fredbird," not "Mr. Dillon."

She knows Mr. Dillon's lying, all right.

Visitors are supposed to buzz in at the main entrance to my old elementary school, but the school office is on the second floor and the only elevator is at the back of the building, so I head there instead.

Mr. Considine, my longtime PE teacher, is standing beside the rear entrance. He seems shocked to see me. "Noah?"

"The one and only," I say.

"How are you doing?" He casts an eye over my top-of-the-line wheelchair. "I mean, you look well." He reddens. "Hey, we've got Fredbird visiting today!"

I put on a surprised face. "The Cardinals' mascot? Here?"

"Yeah. One of the TV announcers is here too. You should come watch."

He waves me inside. I weave past mounds of multicolored book bags and into the gym. Seeing row after row of cross-legged kids reminds me of when I used to go here. But there's one kid who's apart from it all. Someone familiar.

Dynamo Duric sits in his wheelchair next to the far wall. Unless he started at the school in the past year, we must've overlapped for a while, although I don't remember him. Come to think of it, I don't remember seeing anyone in a wheelchair. Then again, since he's doing PT, Dynamo probably hasn't always needed a wheelchair.

Up on stage, Fredbird has wrapped his enormous rubber beak around a kindergartner's head and looks like he's taking a big chomp. Everyone busts out laughing, including Dynamo. Eating kindergartners is clearly a popular elementary school pastime.

As Fredbird bounds across the stage to even louder cheering, I stop thinking about Dynamo and concentrate on the mascot. Three seconds later, I've made some critical observations about everybody's favorite kid-eating bird.

(1) He's as energetic as an Olympic gymnast.

(2) He's as slippery as a snake.

(3) He can jump like a kangaroo.

Let me compare this list to my observations about Mr. Dillon last night at the restaurant.

(1) He gets winded walking to the exit.

(2) He has trouble fitting through doors.

(3) I'd be amazed if he can get both feet off the ground at the same time.

Okay, so numbers 2 and 3 probably seem hypocritical,

coming from me, but I'm in a wheelchair. Plus, I'm not the one pretending to be Fredbird.

A guy I recognize as a Cardinals TV announcer calls for more volunteers. In the middle of the gym, Makayla wiggles her hand about like a flag caught in a tornado. She's bouncing up and down too, which means she's either excited or needs the bathroom.

Unfortunately, the announcer doesn't call on her, and Fredbird doesn't even seem to notice her. But then, maybe that's because *Fredbird isn't her dad.*

I was already feeling bad about the spelling bee disaster, but this might be even worse. She's bursting with pride, like she really believes the athlete in the bird suit is her father. How will she feel when she finds out the truth?

One thing's for sure: I'm not going to be the one to tell her.

Makayla's teacher, Mrs. Coates, is leaning against the wall of the gym, watching me. She was my fourth-grade teacher too, and looks exactly the same as I remember, even down to the bright red *Got Book?* T-shirt. When I give a little wave, she wanders over.

"Noah?" she says like she can't believe her eyes. "What are you doing here?"

"Hi, Mrs. Coates." I swallow hard. "Actually, I—I was

wondering if we could talk. Outside."

She follows me out of the gym. We're alone in the hallway, but that doesn't make it any easier to speak.

"What do you need?" she asks kindly.

I swallow hard. "I, uh, heard you had a practice spelling bee yesterday."

She raises an eyebrow. "How do you know that?"

"Makayla told me."

"You know Makayla?"

"My mom's friends with her dad."

"Ah." Mrs. Coates straightens a flyer on the wall. "Makayla's a really bright kid. You have to be on your A game with her."

"I noticed. She got me into trouble on Friday." I hesitate. "That's the problem, actually."

My old teacher looks lost. "What is?"

I already don't like how this conversation is going, and I'm pretty sure it's about to get worse. "Makayla left her list of spelling words in our house. And I thought it'd be kind of funny to redo the list with the words spelled wrong, you know?" I give a little chuckle, hoping that Mrs. Coates might see the funny side.

Mrs. Coates doesn't see the funny side. "What are you talking about, Noah?"

"I sabotaged Makayla's test!" I blurt out. "I know it was a really bad thing to do, and now I can't sleep. I feel like I'm the worst person in the world."

Mrs. Coates watches me in shocked silence. I wait for her to cuss me out or have me thrown in juvenile detention or maybe a lunatic asylum. The last thing I expect her to do is laugh.

"Uh, Mrs. Coates?"

She tries to stop, but that only makes it worse. Doubled over, she doesn't even hear me. A couple teachers leave the gym and check the hallway to see what's going on. When I shrug, they move along.

Several seconds pass before she gets control of herself. "Oh, Noah," she murmurs. "Noah, Noah, Noah."

"Yes, Mrs. Coates?"

She blinks back tears. "Makayla Dillon got one hundred percent on the test, just like always. It's highly likely she'll be in the school final of the spelling bee . . . just like always."

"But . . ." I try to make sense of it. "I changed the words. I tricked her. She told me she failed so badly that you disqualified her from the bee. She even cried at my birthday dinner. I was so scared she was going to tell my mom what I did, I couldn't even order dessert."

Mrs. Coates wipes away the tears running down her cheeks. "That's terrible," she says like it's the funniest thing she's ever heard. "What about Makayla? Did *she* order dessert?"

Like a fog lifting, the truth slowly dawns on me. And once it's clear, I wonder how I ever missed it. It's as obvious as one of Flub's super-potent farts at close range.

Makayla Dillon *played me*.

I rewind through the past few days. Makayla *wanted* me to hear her practicing spelling words. She even made sure I knew that she was leaving the spelling sheet behind on our kitchen table, and that it was her *only copy*. She *tricked* me into sabotaging her chances, and I fell for it. I even wasted an hour typing carefully misspelled words into my computer.

Mrs. Coates gives me a sympathetic pat on the shoulder. "Like I say, Makayla's as smart as a whip, so you'd better bring your A game. And no offense, Noah, but even that probably won't be enough."

Mrs. Coates returns to her students, leaving me alone in the hallway. In the gym, everyone is laughing again. I'm not laughing, though. I want revenge. I want justice.

This is war!

GIRLS LIKE THE DYNAMO

Mom is leaning against the minivan. Her eyes are closed, and she's facing the sun. She looks relaxed and happy, which doesn't happen very often these days. Then her supersonic hearing picks up the sound of my tires from twenty yards away and she jolts to attention.

"Everything okay, honey?" she asks, watching me.

"Perfect," I lie.

As she leans over and wraps her arms around me, I push hard on the handles of my wheelchair. It helps her a little, but I can still feel the muscles in her shoulders and arms and back straining. What will she do when I'm in high school and weigh fifty pounds more?

It takes her a couple minutes to join me in the car. "You sure you're okay?" she asks again.

What she really means is that it's obvious I'm *not* okay, but I'm not going to tell her why. Makayla declared war on *me*, not *us*. But Mr. Dillon . . . well, that's a different matter.

"Please talk to me, Noah."

I pick at the worn seat in front of me. "Fine. I just saw Fredbird."

"That was the point of going in, right?"

"Mr. Dillon isn't Fredbird, Mom."

She's reaching for the seat belt but freezes. "What do you mean?"

"He can't be. Fredbird's way too athletic."

Mom snaps the seat belt into place. "That's not a nice thing to say, Noah. Very disrespectful, in fact."

"Okay, but . . . you don't actually *believe* Mr. Dillon's Fredbird, do you?"

"Why would he lie?"

"To impress Makayla."

Mom snorts. "Don't be ridiculous."

155

Mom is one of the smartest people I know. I can't believe she's covering for him. "Why doesn't this matter to you?" I ask.

Mom jerks the keys in the ignition. "Because this has nothing to do with Fredbird. I think you just don't like Mr. Dillon."

"Because he's a liar!"

"Enough!" She tucks her hair carefully behind her ears. "Look, Noah, I keep telling you he's just a friend, but with your father gone—"

I jam my hands over my ears. I can't force her to hear the truth about Mr. Dillon, but she can't force me to listen to excuses either. Especially if she's going to mention Mr. Dillon and Dad in the same breath.

When Mom gives up trying to talk, I lower my hands and pick at the seat in front of me again. I even dislodge a piece of foam. It was Dad's seat whenever we took Mom's minivan. He didn't like being a passenger—said there wasn't enough to do—so he'd spend the whole time telling us jokes about people at work. He was a manager at a hardware store, and if you don't think that sounds very funny, you don't know how many ways there are to block a toilet.

For a moment, I feel a smile forming on my lips. But then

I remember that he's gone, and the smile fades away. I can't bring Dad back. But I'll do whatever I can to keep his seat empty.

I'm early to my PT appointment—got to keep the insurance people happy!—but I'm still mad as heck.

Luckily, Angelica is working with another patient, so I sneak off to the bathroom. This is a clever strategy for me because bathroom breaks aren't exactly super quick. If I play my cards right, I can burn through several minutes of my session without having to move a muscle—well, except for the malfunctioning ones in my butt.

Unfortunately, the door is locked. I hope whoever's inside hurries up. If Angelica sees me, the game's up.

I hear the toilet being flushed. The squeak of rubber tires against tile. Shouldn't be long now.

Then the person inside starts . . . rapping.

"Watch me now. Enjoy the show.
People love the Dynamo.
Give it up. Just let it go.
No one beats the Dynamo."

Unbelievable. Even the bathroom isn't safe from him anymore. And don't get me started on Dynamo's voice—he sounds like he's sucked on ten helium balloons.

Anyway, what's he doing here? He was supposed to have PT yesterday. If I'd known he was going to move his appointment too, I might've skipped my birthday dinner for a chance to enjoy PT in peace.

Dynamo emerges from the bathroom and stops dead. "It's my mascot!" he exclaims. "Didn't want to miss this week's episode of The Dynamo Show, huh?"

I roll my eyes. "What are you talking about?"

"*You.* The way you watch me all the time, it's like you're my mascot. Hey, I get it—you like what you see, right?" He nods to himself. "Everybody likes watching the Dynamo."

I ought to say something, but really, where would I start? He's clearly crazy.

He's also blocking the toilet door. I nudge him with my wheelchair, but he doesn't take the hint.

"I guess some kids are just born to lead," he says, tapping his chest. "Others are born to watch."

"Okay, for one thing," I say, "you are *not* a leader. You're a fourth grader. For another thing, mascots don't watch anyone. That's cheerleaders, you moron."

"Right. Cheerleaders," he says like it was his idea all along. "But you're way too ugly to be one of them. And I ought to know, 'cause my sister's on Team Fredbird."

"Team *what*?"

"Fredbird. She's a cheerleader for the Cardinals."

Dynamo is certifiably insane. It's like he thinks that just saying something out loud makes it true. Next he'll be telling me that his dad is the team manager. Worst of all, both of our PTs have seen us now, and they're listening to every word. So why don't they call him on his lies?

"You don't believe me," says Dynamo. "Whatever. Just ask my girlfriend. She'll tell you."

We're back to the imaginary girlfriend again.

"Oh, I get it," he continues. "You're jealous. What can I say? Girls like the Dynamo."

Talking to Dynamo is like talking to Makayla—words fly right back, just faster and multiplied. I'm already exhausted, and I haven't even begun my session yet.

My spiky-haired nemesis turns his wheelchair around and speeds into the waiting arms of his PT. Anyone would think he actually *likes* suffering through round after round with the weight-supporting harness.

Meanwhile, Angelica walks up to me and sits on her haunches. "Have a nice chat?" she asks.

"Sure," I say. "It reminds me how lucky I am not to have a younger brother."

"Hmm. Doesn't mean Dynamo isn't right."

I feel my chest tighten. "You don't actually *believe* that stuff he's saying, do you?"

"About you being his mascot?" She shrugs. "You do spend a lot of time watching him."

"I'm not watching him—"

"*Noah* . . ." Sighing, she takes both my hands in hers. "I think you're hiding how you really feel, like a mascot behind a mask. And sooner or later, you're going to have to take it off." She gives me a sympathetic smile. "Once you show us the real Noah Savino, we can help you get on with the rest of your life. Do you understand?"

Angelica has been giving me pep talks ever since we started working together, and I've managed to ignore almost all of them. But it's hard to ignore someone who's holding your hands and staring right at you. Plus, something feels different today. I'm tired of hearing about how I'm letting myself down. I'm angry that Dynamo thinks he owns me, and I hate that Makayla played me for an idiot. And most of all, I'm sick of all the lying—Mr. Dillon pretending to be Fredbird, and Mom acting like she might believe him.

Maybe I should tell Angelica the truth, for a change. How I've been afraid to try too hard or say out loud what I want in case I can't make it happen. How I figure it's better not to get my hopes up at all than to risk losing hope altogether. How I get that nothing's guaranteed with a spinal injury, and no two people heal exactly the same way, and some people never really heal at all. How I'm scared that's what'll happen to me.

"What are you thinking about, Noah?" Angelica asks gently.

I'm thinking that if I can't turn things around, the insurance will stop paying for PT and I'll never get better. I'll just get older, and heavier, and harder for Mom to handle. Who will she call on when she can't manage me by herself? What will my life look like then?

"Noah?"

I take a deep breath and meet her eyes. "I'm thinking . . . you're right."

Angelica nods, but she doesn't say anything for several

moments. "Okay, then," she says finally. "Let's see how those exercises are coming."

I wheel over to the mat with her. Then, working side by side with my PT, I do something I've never done before.

Exactly what I'm told.

THE BEAST HAS A SOFT SIDE

Mrs. Friendly is wearing her official CrossFit competition vest with "THE BEAST" written in block letters across her muscular upper back. If you ask me, Sam "THE BEAST" Friendly isn't very imaginative as nicknames go. I think she should change it to Sam "I'M NOT VERY" Friendly. She probably wouldn't go for that, though. Mrs. Friendly's sense of humor is not as developed as her biceps.

I'm halfway around the gym, warming up my own pathetic biceps and triceps and all those other upper arm muscles I never knew existed, when she blows her whistle. Everyone grinds to a halt.

"What are you doing, Savino?" she barks.

"Uh . . . I uh . . ." I give her a vacant smile, but The Beast is not easily calmed. "I'm . . . rolling?"

"And why are you rolling?"

"Because I . . . you know . . . my legs don't work." This really shouldn't be news to her. It's not like I've been faking it.

"And so you roll," she says, nodding to herself. "And that's what I like to see, people. Savino's giving it everything. Ask yourself: 'Am I outworking Savino?'"

I hate being singled out. Even a teacher as unfriendly as Mrs. Friendly ought to know that she shouldn't draw attention to my disability. It's why teachers are given sensitivity training. It doesn't matter that she's trying to compliment me—it's a reminder that I'm different from everyone else.

Like I need reminding.

She strides over to Logan. "How about you, Montgomery? Are you outworking Savino?"

Logan is massaging his left knee. "My leg still hurts," he says.

"Your . . . leg . . . still . . . hurts," she repeats like the words don't make sense. "And why does your leg hurt?"

"Because Alyssa threw a baseball at me. You were there! You saw it!"

Mrs. Friendly cocks an eyebrow. "Is that correct, Choo? Were you aiming for Montgomery?"

"No!" says Alyssa. "I pitched to him. He was inadequately prepared for a bouncer, and so the ball became momentarily embedded around his kneecap."

"She hit me!" cries Logan.

Complaining is probably not the best approach to take with a teacher who calls herself The Beast. "Rumor has it you played an entire baseball game this past weekend," Mrs. Friendly says.

"Well . . . yeah."

"That was against other boys," Alyssa points out. "He probably didn't need to work as hard against weaker opposition."

Logan's face is bright red. "Just wait until the rematch. You are going *down!*"

"Like last time? Oh, no, wait—that was you who crumpled into a heap."

As entertaining as it is to watch Alyssa humiliate Logan, it's also giving us a free time-out. Mrs. Friendly doesn't like free time-outs. Mrs. Friendly likes to inflict pain, so she blows her whistle. "Montgomery and Choo—ten more laps. The rest of you, take a break."

Wait, *what?* Mrs. Friendly has never shortened our workout

before. Sometimes, she acts like she's about to take pity on us, but then doubles the punishment as if she's afraid she's getting soft. Does this mean The Beast actually *is* getting soft?

Grimacing, Logan hobbles around the gym as Alyssa glides by smiling. The rest of my class is smiling too . . . even Logan's teammates, although they try to hide it whenever he looks over.

Justin, my former teammate, eyes my wheelchair. "You're getting quicker on that, Noah," he says.

"Quicker than us, anyway," adds Carlos.

I flick the tires. "Gotta love wheels."

They laugh, which feels surprisingly good. Apart from Logan, no one on the baseball team has said much to me since school started.

"How's the rehab going?" Carlos asks.

"Better," I say. "The insurance company won't keep paying for therapy if they don't see results, so I figured I should get off my butt and work harder."

"You're on your butt now," Justin says.

This time, I laugh too.

Alyssa finishes her laps before Logan and heads over to us. She's not even out of breath. "You all right, Noah?" she asks. "Your face is all scrunched up."

"Oh." I try to relax. "I'm, uh, trying to move my left foot."

"The insurance people are going to stop his rehab if he doesn't get better," explains Carlos.

I think he likes having the inside scoop. But that's not exactly what I told him, and it's definitely not a helpful thing to pass along to Alyssa.

She bites her lip. "That's awful."

"Not if I can give them results," I say, focusing all my energy on my foot.

"You should've told me."

"Should've told you what?" asks Dee-Dub, joining us.

"Noah might not be allowed to keep going to rehab anymore," says Alyssa.

That's not accurate either, and everyone is quiet now. I think they want to believe that rehab is a miracle cure, just like I did when I first started. Would they understand if I told them how complicated it really is? How even now, with every ounce of energy focused on my foot, I can't make anything happen?

"I'm serious," murmurs Alyssa. "I could've helped. I could've—" She stops suddenly, and her mouth hangs open. "Uh, Noah? Your foot's moving."

My heart skips a beat. I try to follow her eyes, but it's

impossible to see my feet without leaning way forward, and I don't want to topple over. "Seriously? It moved?"

"Yeah," she says, nodding furiously. "It really did!"

As I try again, Dee-Dub studies my sneaker like it's a cross between a rare flower and an unsolvable equation. "She's right," he says. "Your foot's definitely moving."

For a few seconds, there's stunned silence. Then Justin and Carlos bump fists, and Dee-Dub holds out his hand for me to shake, and Alyssa starts tearing up. I feel like I'm going to cry too. I can't cry, not here, not now, but if I can move my foot, maybe one day I really will move my legs. And if I can move my legs, maybe I'll be able to walk around the gym. I'll probably never run, and Dee-Dub will look like an Olympic sprinter compared to me, but still . . . we're running different races.

I feel like I did when I used to play baseball. The adrenaline rush of calling a pitch on a full count. The excitement of throwing out a runner caught stealing a base. The celebrations after every victory.

I haven't felt like this in months.

A few yards away, Mrs. Friendly signals for me to join her. I race over and stop beside her.

"Everything okay?" she asks.

"I just moved my foot!"

"Score one for Team Savino!" She gives me a high five. "Hey, look I . . . I'm sorry I singled you out just now. I got excited."

I don't think I've ever heard The Beast apologize before. "It's okay. I'm pretty excited too."

"I can see that." She rolls her neck, eyes fixed on Logan still circling the gym. "You know, I talked to your mom at the beginning of the school year. Asked her if she wanted me to make you work. You probably hate me for it, right?"

"I used to. But not anymore."

She gives a triumphant little fist pump. "Excellent!"

The Beast blows her whistle as Logan staggers across the line, his left foot dragging along the floor. "All right, people," she snaps. "We've got work to do."

With a chorus of sighs, my classmates await the next batch of punishment. I do too, although I'm not sighing. I want to get started again. I want to see what I can do.

I've got a race to win.

CRIMINAL MASTERMINDS

Dee-Dub invites me around to his house on Friday evening. He lives a couple miles away near Tower Grove Park, in a three-story brick house that's even older than mine.

He answers the front door and helps me bump up the step into the house. The hardwood floors are shiny, and there are three squares of paint in different shades of beige on the wall beside us. If Mr. and Mrs. Hardesty are decorating, they must be planning to stick around St. Louis for a while, which means Dee-Dub will too. This makes me very happy.

Dee-Dub leads me into the dining room, where an impressive telescope stands by a window.

"Stargazing's not so good in St. Louis," he says, following my eyes. "Too much light pollution. New Mexico had amazing skies, especially outside Albuquerque."

Talking about amazing, his computer station is gigantic. Sprawling across one corner of the room is a desktop tower with about eighty fans and a monitor that's larger than our TV. There are even speakers mounted against the wall. Dee-Dub could probably take over NASA with this gear. Maybe he already has.

"I built it myself," he says. "Mom doesn't like me wearing headphones because she says it's hard to get through to me. So I added an amplifier and surround-sound system instead. That way I can just drown her out."

I've been told that honesty is the best policy, but Dee-Dub's mom is standing in the kitchen doorway watching us. "I heard that," she tells him.

"That's okay," he says. "You're allowed to listen in."

In my house, this would count as snarky or disrespectful, but I don't think Dee-Dub is trying to be either. He's just being honest, even if that includes telling me about the insanely loud speakers designed to block out his parents' voices.

With a deep sigh, Mrs. Hardesty leaves the room.

"I . . . uh . . . need to say sorry," Dee-Dub mumbles. "For getting angry at you in math."

I don't know what he's talking about.

"On Tuesday, remember? You called me the name of a famous Austrian physicist."

"Oh, you mean Einst—" I stop myself just in time. "It's no big deal."

"I never should've gotten angry." He furrows his brows. "I'm supposed to count to ten. I have deep-breathing exercises too."

I think I might be pulling a Ms. Guthrie Mount Rushmore face. Or Mom's *Did-that-smell-come-from-Noah-or-the-dog?* face. "It's okay," I say. "Honestly, I won't say that name ever again. Well, except maybe when I get to high school physics. But can I ask you something?"

"You just did."

"Huh? Oh, yeah. Right. But seriously . . . why are you okay being called Dee-Dub and not, you know, a famous scientist?"

"Because Einstein was an actual living person," he says like it's obvious. "I am clearly not Albert Einstein. But I am definitely twice as wide as the average seventh grader. So one name is accurate, and the other isn't. You see?"

I remember what he said about his nickname being based on "objective data." Since he's not literally Einstein, I guess this makes sense to him. All the same, I feel like he's keeping something from me. So I wait. I want him to be honest with me, but I won't force it. I know what it's like to have people pushing you to be something you're not ready to be.

He takes a seat in front of the computer and stares at his hands, fingers knitted tightly together. "And, well . . . ," he continues, "when people used to call me that name, it was like they were saying that math is all I've got."

"You're really good at it."

"So?" He bites his thumbnail. "I saw this movie once about a violin prodigy. She was playing solo with professional orchestras when she was twelve. So everyone figured that's what she'd always do: play the violin. Because it would be such a waste of her talent if she didn't, you know?"

I wait for the rest of the story. Then it hits me. "Are you saying you don't actually *like* math?"

"No! I love it. I just think it would be cool to surprise people. Like the way you did in PE when you moved your foot."

"Oh. Well, we could easily do that!" I press the brakes on

my wheelchair. "If anyone at school knew how well you swing a baseball bat, they'd be amazed."

"Mr. Riggieri thinks I have power to spare," he says proudly.

"Exactly! And when you get a sneak peek at my glove, you're unstoppable."

Dee-Dub flashes a sly grin. "It helps to know where the ball is going."

"Sure does. It'll help you when you face Logan in the pitch-off rematch too."

His expression darkens. "But Alyssa's batting, not me."

"I'm making an executive decision. I think she should be the pitcher, I'll be the catcher, and you'll be our designated hitter."

It's his chance to bail, but Dee-Dub seems intrigued. "It would be nice to see Logan's face when I hit his pitch for a home run."

"He wouldn't ever bother us again," I say.

Dee-Dub holds out his hand for me to shake, which I guess means we have a deal. I really need to teach him to bump fists instead.

When he's done crushing my fingers, Dee-Dub nudges the mouse on the desk and the computer screen blinks to life.

He's building something on Minecraft, but I can't tell what it is.

"It was cool how you moved your foot yesterday," he says. "I didn't know you could do that."

"Me either. I still don't know how it happened, really. Except I've been practicing more the last few days. My PT got on my case. Said I need to stop hiding behind a mask."

Dee-Dub furrows his brow. "You wear a mask to PT?"

"No! It's just a thing people say. Like, unmask a mascot and you see who's underneath."

"So, you're a *mascot?*"

Geez. "No, Dee-Dub. I'm not a mascot."

As Dee-Dub zooms out from his Minecraft world, I finally recognize what he's building. It's Busch Stadium.

"Oh, I get it!" he exclaims suddenly. "You're saying you *know* a mascot."

The image of Busch Stadium reminds me of Mr. Dillon. "Oh, I know a mascot, all right," I mutter. "Except he's not a mascot at all."

"That doesn't make sense." Dee-Dub turns to face me. He looks so serious, it's almost funny. "Are you okay, Noah? You don't sound very happy."

I'm surprised that he noticed. "Okay, fine. Remember that stuff we found out about Odell Dillon?"

"The refuse consultant?"

"Yeah. So he says he's Fredbird, the Cardinals mascot. But that's clearly a lie, 'cause we already know what he does. Plus, I saw Fredbird at my old elementary school and there's no way Mr. Dillon was inside that suit."

Dee-Dub doesn't respond for several seconds. "Why would someone lie about being a *mascot*?" he asks.

"I don't know. To impress his daughter, I guess. She was at the school too, and Fredbird never even looked at her. It was like he didn't recognize her. Her dad's lying to her, and she doesn't even know it. Which means he's lying to my mom and me too, and I can't do anything about it."

"Yes, you can. It's like you said just now: get a mascot to take off his mask and you see who's underneath. Once everyone finds out it's not Mr. Dillon, the game is up."

I can't tell if Dee-Dub is serious or not. Is he just finding a solution like he does in math? Or is he actually saying we should try to unmask Mr. Dillon?

"So, how would we do it?" I ask, playing along.

Dee-Dub scratches his chin. "Well, there might be more than one Fredbird, so we'd need to pick a day when Mr.

Dillon says he's going to be in the suit."

"He says he's going to be Fredbird at next Friday's Cardinals game. Oh, that reminds me, I've got a couple tickets to the game. Want to go?"

"Next Friday," he repeats like he might have a hundred other things planned for that night. "It's possible, I suppose. But it doesn't give us much time."

"Much time for what?"

"To make it all happen, of course!"

He begins to type furiously—searching keywords like "mascots" and "performance routines," "Busch Stadium" and "security guards." The way his eyes zip across the gigantic monitor, it's like he's taking mental photographs of every page he reads.

"We'll need an operational code name," he says, eyes still fixed on the screen. "How about the Great Mascot Unmasking?"

"Operation GMU?"

He purses his lips. "Hmm. Not a good acronym. How about Operation MUD? Mascot: Unmask and Destroy."

"Whoa! *Destroy?*"

"Too heavy, huh?"

"A little, yeah."

I really don't know what he's doing, but it's fun to watch. Even if it's all for show, I feel like I'm getting a glimpse into the mind of a *real* criminal mastermind instead of a bumbling amateur like Noah the Anti–Spell Check.

Dee-Dub points to the screen as another wave of information flows across it. "Odell Dillon is a refuse consultant, which means he probably has keys to Fredbird's nest."

"Nest?"

"It's what they call his changing room," explains Dee-Dub, reading from a Busch Stadium guide.

"I get it," I say, catching on. "You're saying we should steal Mr. Dillon's keys. Make him late to a game!"

Dee-Dub sighs deeply, like I'm failing in my role as co-criminal. "If Mr. Dillon isn't the mascot, what difference will it make if he's late to a game?" He shakes his head. "No. We need to change the game itself."

"Ah!" I snap my fingers. "You're saying we should hold him *hostage*. That way, everyone will know he's not Fredbird."

Dee-Dub stares at me like I've grown an extra head. "No," he says wearily. "We borrow Mr. Dillon's keys and let ourselves into Fredbird's nest. Then we put itching powder in the mask."

Silence. I wait for Dee-Dub to start laughing. It's obvious

now that he's been joking all along. Which is actually kind of reassuring.

But Dee-Dub doesn't laugh. Does that mean he's actually serious?

"Did you just say . . . *itching powder?*" I ask.

"Yup."

"Is that even a real thing?"

He looks offended. "Of course it's real. You can buy it online. And it works too."

Dee-Dub knows the strangest things.

"While Mr. Dillon is looking for his lost keys," he continues, "the *real* Fredbird will be getting dressed. By the time the mascot is on the field, he'll be getting so itchy he'll have to pull the mask off. When he does, thousands of people will see that the guy underneath isn't Mr. Dillon. Your job is to make sure that his daughter and your mom see it too."

I can't believe what I'm hearing. "You want to unmask Fredbird in the middle of a Cardinals game?"

"Obviously."

"Just to prove Mr. Dillon's a liar?"

After a few moments, Dee-Dub says quietly, "I hate it when people lie. It's hard for me to know when people are being serious or just joking around, but when they lie . . ." He shakes his head. "It's hard for me. That's all."

I understand what he's saying. And it sure would be nice to prove to Mom that I was right about Mr. Dillon. If she could see with her own eyes that he's been lying to Makayla, Mom wouldn't want him to come around our house anymore, that's for sure. He'd be out of my life for good.

The trouble is, Dee-Dub's plan is completely crazy. And now I have to find a way to break it to him gently.

"I don't know," I say. "I've been to a lot of Cardinals games, and I've never seen Fredbird's nest. It could take ages to find it. And in case you haven't noticed, I'm not as mobile as I used to be."

This is supposed to slow him down, but Dee-Dub's on a mission now. As he begins typing again, he has the same determined expression as when he's flying through a problem set in math class. He's not even using a regular search engine. It's like he's writing computer code. It all looks kind of . . . illegal.

Moments later, he downloads a file: "Busch_Stadium_blueprint."

"Uh, Dee-Dub? Are we supposed to see this?"

"Supposed to?" he asks.

I puff out my cheeks. "Is it *legal*?"

"That's hard to say. Coders have a complicated relationship with the concept of proprietary rights."

"No, then."

He stops typing for a moment. "No," he agrees.

I gulp. Dee-Dub really is a criminal mastermind. And he's not done. He opens the file and scans the blueprint.

"Here it is," he says, tapping the desk like he's too excited to keep still. "The official room name of Fredbird's nest is *01.32.04. Fredbird.* It's on the floor below the main concourse. There's even an elevator right around the corner."

"But . . . but it'll be guarded," I say. "They don't let just anyone down there."

"So we'll create a diversion. Tell the guard someone's fallen on the stairs."

"And when they find out we're lying?"

"Who says we'll be lying? I can think of lots of ways to help a small kid fall down the stairs."

"Dee-Dub!"

He pauses. "That was a joke," he says.

"Oh. Ha! That's pretty funny," I say. But my insides are churning. Is he serious about going through with this?

"We'll be in and out before anyone knows what's happening." He pulls up a calendar on his computer, selects Friday,

September 29, and enters: "Operation MUD."

"I thought it was Operation GMU," I say.

He erases "MUD" and writes "GMU." "Happy now?" he asks.

I truly have no idea how to answer that question.

DON'T LITTER

When I was young, Mom used to read me this book about our "fragile" planet. It was like a before-and-after story, with a picture of a crystal clear river on one side of the page and a polluted river on the other. Or a picture of a field on one side and a landfill on the other. I realize now that it was supposed to make me care more about Earth, and it worked. I never toss litter on the ground. I don't know anyone who does. But *someone* must, because one week after we cleaned up Berra Park, the area around the baseball diamond is cluttered with plastic bottles and candy bar wrappers again.

"It'll only take us a few minutes to clear up," says Mr.

Riggieri breezily. He was waiting for us when Alyssa and Dee-Dub and I arrived at ten o'clock sharp. He has baseball gear too, which makes me wonder if this is really about picking up trash or if he's just looking for an excuse to coach us so we never hit his windshield again.

I guess Alyssa is thinking the same thing because she corners me as I fluff up another large black trash bag. "How well do you know Mr. Riggieri?" she whispers.

"Not very well," I admit. "He keeps to himself. Why?"

"I'm not complaining, but it's kind of weird that we broke his windshield and he's not even making us pay for it."

"He said he's insured. Anyway, we're cleaning the park instead."

"That's hardly the same thing." She tilts her head so that her long, dark hair covers one eye. "And now he's coaching us in baseball too. Which is great, but . . . Well, you have to admit it's odd."

Personally, I think Alyssa has an overactive imagination, but I'm smart enough to keep this thought to myself. I've seen how hard Alyssa can throw a baseball, and I want her to keep aiming for my glove, not my head.

For twenty minutes, we pick up all the trash in Berra Park. I don't mind it too much either. It's another clear, sunny day, and there's something satisfying about making a place clean again. Pieces of trash are a real turnoff, but now the ground is clear, and I'm itching to take my place behind home plate.

Mr. Riggieri hands me a mask and mitt and gives Dee-Dub a new bat. I almost forgot that Dee-Dub broke the last one, and Mr. Riggieri doesn't mention it. Which makes me wonder if maybe Alyssa is right when she says there's something weird going on. Why doesn't Mr. Riggieri care that we keep breaking his stuff?

We pick up right where we left off last week. With Dee-Dub watching from the sidelines, Alyssa stares at my glove like she's trying to bore a hole in it. Then she pitches . . . and it's good. Better than good. The control is almost there, and the velocity . . . Let's just say I'm glad I'm wearing a glove.

I move my hand to the corner of the zone, and she pitches again. The ball makes contact a few inches too low, but I know plenty of batters who would've taken a swing at it. She pitches again and again, and after each one, Mr. Riggieri offers a few words of advice or encouragement. He's a patient coach, but I still don't understand how Alyssa Choo became an overnight pitching sensation.

"What's the secret?" I yell to her. "You're not on steroids, are you?"

She rolls her eyes, but it's obvious she likes the compliment. "I've been practicing with my dad," she says, grinning.

"Oh." I try to grin right back at her, but I'm suddenly hit by a feeling of emptiness. My dad and I used to practice together here. Now Alyssa practices with her father. Why didn't she call *me* to work with her instead? Does she think I'm not up to it?

Maybe she just prefers hanging out with her dad, Noah.

Dee-Dub steps to the plate, blocking my view of Alyssa. "Are you okay?" he asks.

I look up. Try to focus. "Yeah. Sure."

On the mound, Alyssa prepares to unleash another pitch. I can tell it's going to be a doozy, but as she winds up, Dee-Dub sneaks a peek at my glove. She lets the ball fly, and sure enough, Dee-Dub hammers it halfway across the park.

Before it comes back down to earth, there's a smattering of applause from just behind us. I crane my neck to look through the chain-link fence. I'm afraid it's going to be Logan again, but it's even worse. Today's fans are none other than Mr. Dillon and Makayla.

Mr. Dillon waves at me. Makayla has a sly look on her face, like she's already planning my next humiliation.

They wouldn't be smiling if they knew about Operation GMU.

Having run halfway across the field to retrieve the baseball, Alyssa is panting as she prepares to pitch again. I try to warn her that she should wait until she catches her breath. If her pitch has less power than usual, Dee-Dub might hit the ball so far we'll never see it again.

But Alyssa doesn't have a slow gear, and when she sees the position of my glove at the bottom right corner of the strike zone, she nods once and prepares to pitch. Dee-Dub glances at the glove too. A moment later, Alyssa delivers the ball.

She's lost some control and leaves the pitch up in the strike zone. It's high enough that any half-competent batter would realize the error and let it rip. But Dee-Dub has already made up his mind where the ball is going. As he swings, he catches only the tiniest bottom edge.

The ball shoots straight up like a rocket. The breeze carries it back a little ways, but it's still above me. I can catch this. I *want* to catch this—not just for Alyssa, who needs a break, but also for *me*. I want to show Mr. Dillon that I don't need his help or anyone else's. I am a catcher. This is what I do.

Left hand on the wheel, I spin myself around and nudge forward a couple yards. The ball is coming down now, and the wind is pushing it farther out of reach. As I propel myself again, I hear Mr. Dillon shouting, "No!" He's rattling the chain-link fence too, to warn me that I'm getting close. I want to yell at him to shut up. I know exactly where the fence is, thank you very much, and there's no way I'll risk hitting it.

The ball is plummeting now, and I'm ready. Well, almost ready. A little clockwise move and another yard forward and—

It all seems to happen at once: Mr. Dillon yelling at me to stop, and my front wheel catching on something I can't see, and my outstretched arm carrying my body forward so that I slide off the chair and crumple to the ground. The chair topples onto me, and the ball lands on my left arm, and I feel so many types of pain, I don't even know which one makes me scream.

Dee-Dub towers over me, blocking out the sun. He looks as horrified as I feel but doesn't have a clue what to do. He doesn't seem to realize the chair is pressing against my legs and I can't get it off me.

A few seconds later, Alyssa kneels beside me. "Are you all right?" she wheezes.

No, I'm not all right. I'm lying on the ground, covered in red dust. I can even taste it in my mouth. I can't move my legs, and I feel like I've been stabbed in my left arm. And I didn't even make the catch.

It's this final thought that does me in. I know it's stupid, and really, *who cares?* But after PE this week, I thought I'd turned a corner.

I wanted to catch that ball so much. I *needed* to.

Alyssa frees my legs, but I can't feel anything. It's like I'm not even me anymore, and I'm just watching the scene play out. And what I see is a pathetic, dusty, crippled kid lying in a heap on the ground as a really cute girl tries to help him, like she's his mom or something. And there's nothing he can do about it, because he's stuck. He's helpless.

That's when I realize I'm crying. I don't *want* to cry, but like everything else, the tears are out of my control. I'm a passenger in my own body, and I freaking hate where it's taking me.

"You'll be all right," Alyssa says in a soothing voice.

"We've got you," says Mr. Riggieri, puffing after his sprint across the diamond.

"Go away!" I yell at them. "Just . . . get away from me."

I try to push myself to a sitting position, but my left arm

buckles under me, and my head hits the ground again. More dust billows into the air, and I breathe it in and spit it out and wonder if my left cheek is bleeding or just bruised.

I'm sobbing now, which completely sucks. The little kids on the playground will be frightened. No one likes to see baseball players getting emotional. I wish everyone would just go away and leave me alone. I wish it had never happened.

I wish so many things had never happened.

I feel arms sliding beneath me. Someone lifts me off the ground. "I've got you," Mr. Dillon says.

I turn my head. His face is only inches away from mine. "Put me down," I growl.

He doesn't take any notice. When Alyssa says there's something wrong with one of my wheels, he swings me over his shoulder like a fireman and begins to walk in the direction of home. "It's okay, son," he says. "I've got you now."

"I am not your son!" I shout. "And you're not my dad."

He doesn't reply, so I hit him. It's not a nice thing to do, and because I'm dangling several feet above the ground, it's not very smart either. But once I start, I can't stop. I just keep pounding my fists against his meaty back.

He inhales sharply with every punch, but he never stops walking. "It's okay," he keeps saying. "It's okay."

And I keep yelling back, "I. Am. Not. Your. Son." I never actually say the words "and I never will be," but I think he gets the message because when we arrive home a few minutes later, he lays me gently on the sofa and turns away.

"What happened, Odell?" Mom asks, a stricken expression on her face.

But Mr. Dillon doesn't answer. Just passes her without a word and leaves the room. In this moment, I'm praying that he never comes back. And it's possible my prayers will be answered, because from the look on his face, I'm not the only one who's been crying.

THE RIDDLE OF MR. RIGGIERI

After checking that my arm is just banged up, not actually broken, Mom helps me get to my bedroom. For the rest of the day, I lie on my bed and stare at the blue walls and the tacked-up posters of Cardinals players.

Mr. Dillon comes over in the afternoon. He and Mom try to talk quietly, but I hear his deep voice through the wall. The name Riggieri comes up a few times, but I can't make out much else. I can imagine what they're both saying, though: *Noah is so much work. . . . Noah never appreciates help. . . . Noah Noah Noah blah blah blah . . .*

They're right too. There, I admitted it. I *am* a lot of work, and I *don't* appreciate Mr. Dillon's help, and I hate feeling guilty when I never asked for help in the first place. If Mom wants me to be happy again, she could start by making things the way they used to be. Sure, I should've worked harder at physical therapy, but I'm trying to fix that now. Having Mr. Dillon around isn't helping.

Dee-Dub's plans for Operation GMU don't seem so crazy anymore.

I close my eyes and imagine Dad bursting into the room and announcing that he's kicked Mr. Dillon halfway down the street. Okay, fine, Mr. Dillon's much bigger than Dad, but in my mind, that doesn't matter. Dad can do anything. He can whistle loud enough to overpower a vacuum cleaner. He can fry three eggs at once and make all the yolks different textures, even if he doesn't mean to. He can talk, talk, talk . . . like there's never too much to say. Like there's never enough time to say everything.

The daydream fizzles out. Turns out, that last part was true: there wasn't enough time for us after all.

I wipe my sleeve across my bleary eyes and sniffling nose and reach for the box of baseball cards on my nightstand. They're Dad's rookie cards really, not mine, but it's not like he has any use for them anymore. I used to look at them every day when I was in the hospital. I tried to remember all the stories Dad told me about the players I never got to see, like Ozzie Smith and Mark McGwire. Sometimes I'd forget a detail, and I'd lie in bed and wonder if it meant that I'd forget about Dad one day too.

There's a gap of about six years in his card collection. That's when Dad stopped following baseball because he was focused on me. Then there are the newer cards—Michael Wacha and Carlos Martinez, Matt Carpenter and Kolten Wong—because we'd started to go to Cardinals games together.

We used to sit in the cheap seats and share a hot dog and he'd point to each player and tell me all about him. How Matt Carpenter started as a thirteenth-round draft pick and worked his way through the minor leagues to crack the starting lineup. The way Dad saw it, anyone could make it in baseball with enough hard work and love for the game. "Time and effort, Noah," he used to say. "It's all just time and effort."

I believed him too because I could see it playing out on the field right in front of me. I saw it in every diving catch, and double play, and force-out. Nothing was given, and everything was earned. Who couldn't respect that?

The accident changed all that. Working hard in the

neurorehab center revealed as much about what I couldn't do as what I could, and who wants to know what they *can't* do? So I put in the time but not the effort. Angelica kept pushing, and I kept pushing back. Until this week, anyway. This week, I finally *tried*.

And look where it got me: facedown in the dirt at my neighborhood park.

Dad was wrong. Time and effort don't make everything possible, and not everyone can make it to the major leagues. Some people never get to pick up a baseball, and others can't even stand without help. Some of us get carried through the neighborhood like a rolled-up rug.

How will time and effort fix that?

The next morning, Mom bangs on the door at eight o'clock. I don't answer, but she comes in anyway. She's carrying a plate loaded with pancakes, which is completely impossible to resist, partly because pancakes are my favorite breakfast food but mostly because I'm starving.

I push myself up in bed and tuck in as Mom flashes an anxious smile.

"Thank you," I mumble. "I'll get up soon."

It's my cue for her to leave, but instead, she perches at the end of my bed and rests her hand on my leg hidden beneath the comforter. "You want to talk about what happened yesterday?" she asks.

I try to put on my best thoughtful expression, but I'm chewing so hard, I probably look like a constipated chipmunk. "Not really," I say around a mouthful of pancake.

She moves her hand. It's strange, but the only time we touch anymore is when she's helping me in and out of the car. I wonder if that will ever change.

Mom stands and begins pacing back and forth across the room. It's like watching a zoo animal stuck in a tiny pen. It reminds me of the photo taped above my desk: Dad and me at the Saint Louis Zoo a couple years ago. It took Mom two minutes to snap that picture because Dad was busy dealing with an issue at work. By the time he was done, the elephant that had been standing right behind us was out of the picture. Mom asked Dad to turn the phone off, but he said he couldn't. He did put it away, though.

Mom follows my eyes. "Remember what happened just after that photo?"

She's talking about how the elephant returned with a trunk full of water and sprayed the crowd. Dad got the brunt of it, and we all laughed like crazy.

But she didn't see what happened next. How Dad pulled out his phone to check it was still working. I'll never forget his look of relief when he found out it was okay. I think that might have been the highlight of the trip for him.

"What happened yesterday, Noah?" Mom asks.

I take another bite. "I fell over."

"Hmm. That must've been scary. Bet it hurt too."

Hurt. I never realized how vague that word is, and how many different kinds of pain there are. A hangnail hurts but not the same as what I'm feeling now.

I wait for her to ask me why I went crazy and started hitting Mr. Dillon. Instead, she says, "Mr. Dillon fixed your wheel for you."

Oh, great. So now I'm supposed to be grateful that he's as handy as Dad?

I imagine a barrier falling between us, like the metal screen that Dad lowered outside the hardware store at the end of each day. I take another bite so I won't have to say anything. Speaking will only make things worse.

"Look, I know things are hard for you, honey," Mom says, wringing her hands. "But Mr. Dillon just wants to help. He's trying, you know."

"Yes," I reply. "Very trying."

She grits her teeth so that her jaw muscles bulge. She seems to be forgetting the whole *avoidance* part of conflict avoidance. "What has he done that's so bad, huh? Just tell me that."

"You spend more time with him than you do with me."

"That's not true! And since when do you care? All you ever do is play with the computer. When was the last time you actually talked to me?"

"So, that's what this is about? You want someone to talk to?"

"Yes! You're not the only one who's lonely, Noah. You're not the only one who needs a shoulder to cry on."

Is that supposed to make me feel better? Now all I can think about is Mom crying and Mr. Dillon comforting her.

"He's a liar, Mom!"

"Not this again." She hangs her head. "What do you want me to say, Noah? 'Cause I'm at the end of my rope here. A part of me wants to tell you to stop whining and grow up. I'd do it too, but then I think about Mr. Riggieri and . . ." She waves her hands vaguely through the air.

"What about Mr. Riggieri? I like him."

"Of course you do," she says bitterly. "Because he's nice to you, just like Mr. Dillon is trying to be nice to you. The difference is, Mr. Dillon isn't being nice to other people's kids just to make up for screwing up so badly with his own!"

She stops moving and places her hand over her mouth like she can't believe she just said that.

Come to think of it, neither can I. "I never knew that," I say. "I didn't even know he has kids."

Mom looks like she wants to rewind the conversation. Go back to the part where we were discussing Mr. Dillon's kindness and my ungratefulness. But we've moved on to Mr. Riggieri now, and I need answers.

"How come I never knew that?" I ask.

Mom runs a finger across my chest of drawers. "He has two daughters and a son. They're all grown up now." She stares at the dust coating her fingertip. "His son, Marco, was a very good baseball player in high school. The two of them used to practice in Berra Park. I'd see them when I took you to the playground as a baby." She smiles like it's a happy memory, but the smile doesn't last. "Mr. Riggieri wasn't a nice man back then, Noah. He spent most of his time chewing Marco out. His daughters left home the first chance they got. Marco followed them out the day he graduated high school."

I've never seen anyone visiting Mr. Riggieri's house, but

I figured it was because he didn't have any family. I've only hung out with him a couple times, but I can't believe he was ever as mean as Mom says.

"His kids must've gone a long way away," I tell her, "seeing as how they never visit."

She opens my blinds, and I squint in the bright sunshine. "Actually," she says, staring across the street at Mr. Riggieri's house, "they live right here on The Hill. I still see them around. They always wave and say hi to me. But they never come onto our block."

She turns back to me and sees the plate of half-eaten pancakes. "Eat up, won't you?"

I've lost my appetite. But it's a peace offering, so I take a bite anyway. Chew and chew, even though the pancake tastes dry now.

"I know you miss your dad, honey," Mom says, her eyes moist, "but that doesn't make Mr. Dillon a bad man. Compared to Mr. Riggieri, he's a saint. If only you'd give him the same chance you give Mr. Riggieri, I think you'd see it too."

A part of me still wants to convince her that Mr. Dillon really is a liar. But maybe she's got a point. Maybe that's not the real problem here. I mean, there are probably millions of nice guys in the world, and Mom and I don't need any of them in our lives either.

Even the nicest guys sometimes leave.

I've got a photo above my desk to prove it.

MONSTER TRUCK SPEAKS

On Monday morning, Dee-Dub takes the seat next to me in homeroom. I can tell he wants to say something, but Ms. Guthrie is about to take attendance. One by one we mumble that we're present.

When the bell goes, half-asleep students stagger out of the room. Ms. Guthrie leaves too. Not Dee-Dub, though. First period will be starting soon, but he stays behind, my own private shadow. So does Alyssa. It feels a little like being double-teamed in basketball.

When we're alone, Dee-Dub says, "I need to apologize."

"For what?" I ask.

"On Saturday, when you fell over . . . I panicked. I wasn't sure if it was safe to move you."

I don't want to talk about it, but Dee-Dub won't let it drop until I forgive him. So I say, "It wasn't your fault."

"No," he agrees, "but I didn't respond appropriately. My parents suggested that I read a book on paraplegia—"

"It's not your fault! How many times do I have to say it?"

Dee-Dub glances at Alyssa, who returns a thin-lipped smile. "It would really help me if we could talk, Noah," he says.

"We are talking," I point out.

"No. *Real* talking. Where we tell each other the truth."

"When did I lie?"

He tugs at the collar of his polo shirt like it's suddenly gotten hot. "You never told me you were paralyzed in the same accident that killed your dad. Or that it was his fault."

"What are you talking about?"

"He was looking at his cell phone, wasn't he? And that's why you're in a wheelchair now."

The words hit me like a punch to the gut. I stare at Alyssa, but she looks away. She knew that Dee-Dub was going to ask me about this. She was probably the one who set him up to do it.

I try to leave, but Dee-Dub is blocking my way.

"It's like I told you on Friday," he says. "It's really hard for me when people don't tell the truth."

"We're going to be late for math!"

He doesn't move. "Are you crying?"

"No!"

"There are tears running down your face."

I run my sleeve across my cheeks.

Alyssa slides off her desk and places a hand on Dee-Dub's shoulder. "Hey," she says. "Can you let Noah and me talk for a moment?"

He nods, but he still doesn't budge.

"*Alone*," says Alyssa.

"Oh." Dee-Dub shifts his weight from foot to foot. "Okay."

Alyssa watches him go. "He's just trying to understand, Noah."

"Why did you tell him about the accident?" I hiss.

"I didn't tell him anything! In case you haven't noticed, Dee-Dub's pretty smart. Are you really surprised that he knows how to stick your name in a search engine?" She bites her lip. "Your crash was all over the news. Honestly, I'm kind of amazed it took him this long to work out the details."

I want to be angry with her, and Dee-Dub too, but I know

she's telling the truth. I'm the liar, keeping secrets and pretending I'm not crying when I can feel the tears burning my cheeks. I hate that Alyssa is seeing me this way, just like she did on Saturday. I've had months to get a grip on what happened to Dad and me. Am I still going to be crying in a year? Two years? Why hasn't it gotten easier? Why can't anyone tell me when it'll stop?

"I just liked having one person who didn't know everything about the accident," I tell her. "Someone who's only seen me like this, instead of comparing me to the person I used to be." I stare at my legs. "You probably think I'm stupid."

"No." She takes a seat beside me. "And I don't think Dee-Dub does either. Actually, I think he might feel the same way. We talked for quite a while on Saturday, and things weren't always good for him in Albuquerque. Anyway," she says with a little shake of her head, "we wouldn't hang out with you every Saturday if we thought you were stupid."

"You don't have much choice. Mr. Riggieri said if you didn't show, he'd track you down and murder you in your sleep." Saying the words aloud reminds me of what Mom told me about Mr. Riggieri and his estranged kids. Did he used to joke with them too, or did his threats feel more real back then?

Alyssa touches my arm gently, bringing me back to the present. "That would definitely be a bad way to go," she says. "But Mr. Riggieri isn't the one telling me to hang out with you every lunchtime as well. And he wasn't the reason we hung out all the time in elementary school either."

I look at her hand. My skin tingles. Alyssa's the one good thing that came from the accident, I guess, because I probably wouldn't have ditched Logan and Co. otherwise.

Unfortunately, Logan chooses this moment to return. He lumbers into the room, sees Alyssa and me, and stops abruptly. "Whoa. Are you *crying*, Savino?" He curls his upper lip. "So what if Choo doesn't want to date you? You're too good for her anyway."

Alyssa pulls her hand away. I feel the empty space where she was touching me.

Logan heads back to the desk where he sits during homeroom. Bending over, he picks up his cell phone. "Lucky me," he says. "Thought I'd lost it."

Just seeing the phone makes me tense. When he holds it up and pretends to take a picture of Alyssa and me, I raise my arms to cover my face.

"Geez, Logan," Alyssa huffs as Logan closes in on us. "Just for once, can you stop being such a jerk?"

"Hey, you're the one who broke his heart, not me." He raises his phone again, and this time I'm pretty sure he takes a real photo of us. "I'll send you a copy if you like. You can use it in the yearbook."

"Shut up!" Alyssa yells.

Dee-Dub reappears in the doorway.

Logan sees him and laughs. "I wondered how long it'd be before you came in. I saw you waiting for your boyfriend outside the door."

"Noah's not my boyfriend," says Dee-Dub.

"Whatever." Logan flicks his head. "Why don't you get in the photo with them? Then I could get a picture of Noah with his ex-girlfriend *and* his boyfriend."

"He's not my boyfriend," mutters Dee-Dub. He has no idea that he's making things worse. Arguing with Logan is like using gasoline to put out a fire.

"Go on," says Logan. "It'd be a photo for the ages: short, tall, and wide. Hey, you could be a comedy group."

Alyssa and I don't respond, so Logan approaches Dee-Dub. He holds his phone up, snapping away. "Oh, yeah." He chuckles. "Now we're really working in three dimensions."

Dee-Dub steps back.

"What, no weird comment?" continues Logan. "Isn't this

where you normally spew some crazy stuff that makes no sense to anyone?"

That's the final straw. "Shut up, Logan!" I shout.

He flashes me a smug grin. "Or what? You'll leap up and hit me?"

"Shut. Up!" yells Dee-Dub.

Logan roars with laughter. "Monster Truck speaks!"

Bam! It's like watching a viper attack. One moment, Dee-Dub is as stationary as a hibernating bear, and the next, he tackles Logan. Both of them crash to the ground.

Alyssa flies from her chair and wraps her arms around Dee-Dub, trying to pull him away. But Dee-Dub is too heavy and strong. When she hangs on to him, he rises like the Incredible Hulk and they tumble backward.

Alyssa's head collides against the corner of the teacher's desk with a sickening crack and snaps forward. By the time she hits the floor, she's out cold.

Logan is lying on his side, whimpering. His nose is bleeding like a leaky faucet.

I try to get to them, but there's a maze of classroom furniture in the way. I feel frozen, just taking it all in. Dee-Dub seems frozen too. But then he looks at me, and I look at him, and like he's snapping out of a trance, he begins to cry.

"I don't want to move schools again," he whimpers. "Please, don't make me move again."

Suddenly, Ruben "Dee-Dub" Hardesty's strange world begins to make sense to me. Too late, I understand what Alyssa meant when she said I'm not the only one who wants a chance to start over.

But as the saying goes, the past always catches up to us eventually.

Following the shouts and screams, students run from the hallway and into our classroom. When they see Alyssa and Logan, they begin hollering for a teacher.

That's when I forget about the past altogether. Who cares about it when the future looks so gloomy?

28

GOOD PRINCIPAL, BAD COP

I like Principal Mahoney. He's a good guy. True, he has less hair than a naked mole rat and a smile that makes him look deranged, but hey, if I were in charge of Wellspring Middle School, I'd probably pull my hair out and look bonkers too.

The way he always seems so tired makes me want to be honest with him, just to make his life a little easier. But today, that's not an option.

He tells me that Alyssa's parents have picked her up from school and that Logan and Dee-Dub have been suspended for fighting. He doesn't say how long they're suspended for, but I get the feeling it's not just one day. And that's the problem, right there—I think he's waiting to hear my side of the story before deciding on their final punishments.

"So, tell me what happened this morning, Noah," he says in his friendliest voice.

"Alyssa hit her head," I say.

"Yes, I'm aware of that. But I was hoping you could tell me *how* she hit her head and why Logan's nose is broken."

I frown. I don't mean to, but it sort of happens. I didn't know that Logan's nose is broken. It seems a much bigger deal than a straightforward bloody nose. It also means that Dee-Dub is officially in deep doo-doo.

Principal Mahoney leans across his desk and knits his hands together like he's about to pray. "I want you to know that you're not the one in trouble here, Noah."

"Right. Because I didn't actually do anything," I reply. Which is, conveniently, the truth. I couldn't even help Alyssa for about two minutes because Dee-Dub and Logan's battle shifted the teacher's desk and it was blocking me.

"But you saw everything, didn't you?" he says.

I'm getting Good Cop Mahoney, but Bad Cop Mahoney is hovering in the background. I can see it in his eyes. There's a lot of punishment to be handed out, and he wants it to go to the guilty students.

But who is really guilty here?

"You're not going to expel anyone, are you?" I ask.

Principal Mahoney hesitates, which I guess means yes. "This is a serious matter. I understand that Ruben is your friend, and that's wonderful, but I need to know *exactly* what happened."

I shrink in my chair. "What did the others tell you?"

"Alyssa didn't tell me anything because she *couldn't*. She was concussed and needed to go to the hospital. I'm sure you must feel very bad for her."

Unbelievable! He's avoiding the question *and* trying to make me feel guilty. Of course I feel bad for her. She's my friend, and anyway, none of this is her fault. But still . . .

"What about Dee-Du—I mean, Ruben?" I ask. "What did he tell you?"

"Nothing," replies Principal Mahoney impatiently. "Now I want to hear *your* side."

"What about Logan?"

"Noah!"

I swallow hard. I'm not used to spending quality time in the principal's office, and I don't want to be here now. But if Dee-Dub is about to get kicked out of school, it's not going to be me spilling the beans.

"I'm not really sure I saw anything," I say. "Maybe if you told me what Logan said, it might jog my memory."

I brace myself for full-on Bad Cop Mahoney. Or Chief Punisher Mahoney. Or even Ballistic Missile Mahoney. But he must think I'm braver than I really am, because he backs down. "Okay, fine. Logan says that he was taunting you and Ruben and Alyssa, and—"

"Yes," I say quickly, because I like this version of events. "That's exactly what happened."

"Right. But that still doesn't tell me who started the fight."

I can't stall the guy forever, but as I replay his words, I realize that he told me something important. If Principal Mahoney doesn't know who started it, Logan didn't tell him. I don't know *why* Logan didn't tell him, but it might be the difference between Dee-Dub getting suspended and being expelled.

"I, uh, couldn't really see," I say finally. "Alyssa was in my way."

Principal Mahoney narrows his eyes. Bad Cop is about to make another special guest appearance. "That's very convenient," he mutters.

"Not really. If only I could've seen what happened, I'd be able to help you." I give him a closed-mouth smile, but he doesn't smile back.

"You must've seen what happened to Alyssa, though, right?" he asks.

"Yeah. Like I say, she hit her head."

"Do you know how?"

"No. But I'd like to."

Principal Mahoney is making a strange sound at the back of his throat. I don't think it's a happy sound. "She claims that she tripped, Noah. *Tripped!*" he adds, like it's the craziest thing he's ever heard. Which, come to think of it, it might be.

"Uh, just now you said she didn't tell you anything," I remind him. "You know, because she was concussed."

He grabs a pencil like he's about to write Dee-Dub's death warrant. Then he snaps it in two. "I don't want bullies in my school, Savino! No matter how smart they are."

"I don't think you have to worry about bullying anymore," I assure him. "After today, Logan will know better than to go around running his mouth."

"I'm not talking about Logan! Ruben just sent two of my students to the hospital. I don't want anyone else to follow them. So, if he's a danger to others, you've got to tell me."

It's his final play. He's appealing to my sense of justice and also warning me that it'll be partly my fault if anything happens to anyone else in the future. But he's missing the point: Dee-Dub never would've been in that room if it weren't for me. If I'd just told him about the car accident in the first place, we could've avoided the whole situation. Instead, I pushed him away, and even then he stuck around to support me. How can I turn my back on him now?

"Alyssa is concussed," says Principal Mahoney pleadingly. "Logan's nose is broken!"

I swallow hard. Concussion is a big deal. So is a broken nose. I picture Logan, his swollen schnoz bent back at a weird angle like on one of those crazy-looking tropical birds at the zoo, the ones that spend all day squawking and pooping. I read somewhere that they have remarkably small brains, so I guess Logan has that in common with them too.

I can't help it—as I picture those stupid, screeching, poop-producing birds, a smile begins to play on my lips. This is not a funny situation, and I do *not* want to snort in front of Principal Mahoney. . . .

The snort comes out anyway. I try to make it look like a sneeze and even wipe my nose for effect, but my principal isn't fooled.

"Did you just *laugh*?" he demands. "For heaven's sake, we're talking about the poor boy's nose!"

That does it. The image of Logan's supersized schnoz dances through my mind again. Now I'm laughing so hard, there are actual tears. "It couldn't happen to a nicer guy," I say.

Principal Mahoney leans back in his chair and gives a little smile too. Then he hits me with my first-ever detention.

Oh, well. I guess I had it coming.

IF LIFE HAD DO-OVERS

Detention, it turns out, is not much fun for beginners. Maybe when you've had a few, you build a healthy prisoner-guard relationship with the teachers. But I'm new to it, and the three teachers who take turns to babysit me all seem really disappointed.

Kind of like Mom, actually. She's not impressed by my new bad-boy reputation either. She didn't earn her black belt in conflict avoidance by starting a fight with her middle school principal, that's for sure. And by the time Principal Mahoney lets me out of school, she has visited the school office, found out everything that's gone on today, waited a full hour, and been forced to reschedule my PT appointment.

None of these things makes her happy.

We travel home in silence. When we arrive, Mom yanks my wheelchair from the back, slams the rear door, and comes around the side of the car to glare at me. "I'm still waiting for an apology," she snaps.

Over her shoulder, I can see Mr. Riggieri watching us from his porch. "I already told you," I say, "I didn't have a choice."

"And I'm telling you: I. Don't. Care!"

"I've noticed."

I think Mom would like to pull a Dee-Dub on me right now and toss me in the garbage, but she's as gentle as ever as she helps me out of the car and into my wheelchair. She massages her lower back as she straightens, and I feel bad.

I'm about to apologize to her when she storms off. Even worse, as she reaches the front door, she slides the wooden ramp onto the porch like she's raising a drawbridge.

"What are you doing?" I shout. "I need the ramp to get up."

"No. What you need is a little air. And I need some space."

She steps inside and slams the front door behind her.

It's bad enough that she's not going to help me. But to make it impossible for me to get inside is . . . is . . .

"You've got to respect your mom, Noah!" Mr. Riggieri

shouts from across the street. "Always got to respect a parent."

He's rocking back and forth, and he looks like he just woke up from a nap. The skin around his mouth is particularly red and saggy, kind of like an aging bloodhound.

If I could still use my legs, I'd run up to his house and tell him what I think about respect. But I settle for wheeling myself across the street and calling out to him from the sidewalk instead. "And what about *parents*, Mr. Riggieri? Do they have to respect their *kids*?"

"Only if the kid earns it."

"*Earns* it? No wonder your kids hate you."

He pulls himself out of his seat and stomps to the front of his porch. Stooped over, hands resting on the rail, he looks really old. And really angry.

"What did you say to me, boy?"

"Why didn't you tell me you've got kids?"

He glances from right to left. He's probably not happy about having this conversation out on the street. Well, too bad. I can't climb the steps to his porch, and Mom has shut me out. This is the only place left.

"What does it matter to you?" he growls.

"You never really talked to me before my dad died, but now

you do. And when we broke your windshield, you let us off. Why?"

He's silent for a moment, just glaring at me. Then his shoulders relax. "You can't get up here without help, right?" he asks, rapping his knuckles against the porch railing.

"Right."

I don't think he's strong enough to help me get up those three steps. They probably seem bigger every year when you're as old as he is.

"Let's take a walk," he says.

He grips the rail and takes one step at a time. When he's beside me, we trundle slowly along the sidewalk.

"Who told you?" he asks. "About my kids."

"My mom."

"Did she now?" He smiles to himself. "One day, you're yelling at poor Odell Dillon that he's not your dad; the next, your mom tells you I'm a terrible father. Quite a coincidence."

"I don't want to talk about him," I say. "I want to know what happened between you and your kids."

"Why?"

"Because . . ." I'm not actually sure how to answer that. I'm curious, but it's more than that. I'm angry too. "Because it doesn't make any sense. For them to be so close and you still never see them. If my dad were still around, nothing would keep us apart."

We turn left. I don't know if either of us is thinking about Berra Park, but that's where we're heading.

"What did your mom tell you?" he asks.

"That you were mean when you practiced baseball with your son."

Another little smile, but this time it seems sad. "That's an understatement. Marco had the talent to be great, but he was lazy. That's what I thought, anyway. Now I think he just didn't love the game the way I do."

I hesitate. "That's it? That's why you don't see each other anymore?"

"There were other things too. Things I said. Things I can't take back." He waits for me as I bump down a curb, cross the road, and bump up the other side. "Anyway, it's too late to fix now."

"No, it's not! Just tell him you're sorry."

"I've tried. Some words aren't easy to undo. You might want to remember that."

We continue in silence to Berra Park. It's strange to be back here after Saturday's nightmare. My pulse is faster than usual, and my palms are sweaty. It's not the pain I'm reliving either. It's the humiliation. The shame. And the fear that it could happen again.

Some older kids are using the baseball diamond, so we stop at the edge of the playground and watch them. They're pretty full of themselves, and I'd take Alyssa and Dee-Dub over them any day. If my friends are still able to play, that is.

Mr. Riggieri watches me from the corner of his eye. "You okay? Seem to have a lot on your mind."

"Why are you being so nice to *me*?" I ask.

The question catches him off guard. He looks away and stares at the baseball diamond, his eyes tracing the line from home plate to first base, and second, third, and home again, as if he's imagining a home run.

"Your father was a good man, Noah. Always ready to help people. Like, when my waste disposal blocked last year, he came over that night and got it working again." He nods to himself. "I envied him, actually. The relationship he had with you and your mother. Every time I saw you all, I couldn't help thinking about what I'd lost."

"You haven't *lost* your kids, Mr. Riggieri. They live on The Hill."

"I know, but . . ." He stuffs his hands in his pockets and sighs. "You're right. They do."

"And I'd do anything to spend another day with my dad."

"I know you would."

I take a couple deep breaths. What would I tell Dad about first if he were here right now? My genius best friend? How Alyssa and I are closer than we've ever been? There's so much to say, but Mr. Riggieri isn't my dad. And neither is Mr. Dillon.

He lays a hand on my shoulder. "It's tough, isn't it? Being apart from someone you love."

"Yeah," I say, although I don't think he's just talking about my dad and me anymore. "Just so you know: if you were my dad, I'd still want you around."

He squeezes my shoulder. "And if you were my son, I'd be proud. But no one will ever take your dad's place. No sensible man would try. I'd just like to see you smile again from time to time. You've got a lot of life still to live."

"So do you," I remind him.

We begin the journey back home. It's uphill, and I'm still feeling a little beaten-up from Saturday's accident at home plate, but I won't let it show. Mr. Riggieri is probably finding it tough going too, and he won't let it show either. We're pushing each other in more ways than one.

The long, slow climb gives me time to think. About fathers

and sons, and wasted opportunities. About the things we can't change and the things we can.

Especially the things we can.

As we head along Elizabeth Avenue, I can see that Mom has replaced the ramp by the steps. It's not exactly a flashing neon sign that says "You're forgiven, Noah," but it's as close as I can expect, seeing as how I got a detention and Mom had to sit around waiting for me. So I say goodbye to Mr. Riggieri and wheel up to the front door.

Once I'm inside, I head straight for the computer. When Dee-Dub was here, he found Mr. Dillon's address with a single search. I scroll through the browser history until I find the site he was using, and click on it.

Using only one finger, I type the words "Riggieri Elizabeth Avenue" and hit Enter. A moment later, I have my first result.

Age: 65–69

Current: St. Louis, MO

Knows: Marco Riggieri, Camilla Berrios,
Elena Cohen

Marco is Mr. Riggieri's son. Camilla and Elena might be his daughters. When I click on Marco's name, the site links to a new address on Botanical.

Botanical? That's just the next block over. How can two people possibly avoid each other when they live so close? And why? Really, *why?* I get that Mr. Riggieri was mean, but he's changed. He wants to be forgiven. And if his son and daughters are too stubborn to realize it, then maybe someone needs to help them understand.

I can feel a new plan coming together—another unmasking, except this time, it involves Mr. Riggieri.

And this is one operation I plan on carrying out alone.

ONE IS THE LONELIEST NUMBER

Tuesday. Dee-Dub and Logan are suspended, and Alyssa is staying home. I'm attracting a whole lot of attention again, only this time it's because I was the lone witness to Hardesty vs. Montgomery, the greatest heavyweight prize-fight in Wellspring Middle School history.

All day long, students ask me for details of what went down. I keep it simple in case one of them is a snitch for Principal Mahoney. "Only one kid got a broken nose," I say.

I don't think anyone will mess with Dee-Dub again.

After the final bell, Mr. Kostas stops me in the hallway. "A word, please, Mr. Savino," he says, directing me into an empty classroom.

Held behind two days in a row—Mom won't be pleased.

"So how did you enjoy your first detention yesterday?" he asks.

I redden. "I was out of line."

"Hmm." He perches on the edge of his desk. "How's Alyssa doing?"

"I don't know. I called last night, but her mom said she was sleeping."

"She'll probably be back tomorrow."

"What about Ruben? Will he be back too?"

Mr. Kostas rolls up some sheets of paper and raps them rhythmically against his open palm. "From what I've heard, no. He won't be back until next week."

"Next *week*?"

"I think he needs some time away, Noah. But I was hoping you could give him these work sheets."

He hands over the rolled-up pages. I can't help stealing a glance at the top sheet, but no matter—I think Mr. Kostas expects me to look. And what I see is line after line of really advanced baseball statistics. Not just batting averages but the kinds of metrics that experts use: abbreviations like WHIP and WAR and OPS.

"What do you want him to do?" I ask.

"I want him to decide which of these categories is the most useful and why. Then I want him to create his own."

I blink twice. "Seriously?"

"You've seen his work, Noah. Yes, he's a rather perplexing young man, but Mr. Hardesty is a rare find."

"He does your work sheets in his head. Like, it's automatic for him."

Mr. Kostas gives a small sad smile. "I know. He's quite extraordinary. I want to see him succeed here, but that'll take patience. I could use some help too. Will you help me?"

I look at the sheets again. Of course I want to help, but if yesterday's events proved anything, it's that I'm powerless when Dee-Dub begins to unravel.

Mr. Kostas knits his fingers together. "I've been teaching for thirty years. I've had students like Ruben before. They can be the most enthusiastic and also the most disruptive. They can be the brightest and also the most stubborn. Sometimes you want to hug them; other times you want to yell at them. They're not trying to make life difficult—sometimes that's just how life is for them."

That's just how life is. Mr. Kostas is talking about Dee-Dub, but he could be talking about me too. Since school started, I've felt so angry. I get tense when kids leave their chairs in the aisle so I can't wheel past. I get annoyed when there's a stupid little step and I have to ask for help to get over it. I hate feeling helpless, and I hate being pitied. Most of all, I hate feeling like I'm not in control of my life.

I think maybe Dee-Dub feels that way too.

But Dee-Dub has made me feel normal when other people stared at me. There must be a way for me to help him back.

"I'll do whatever I can," I say finally.

Mr. Kostas beams. "I knew you'd say that. You're a good kid, Noah."

"Thanks. You're a good teacher."

"Hmm. Perhaps you could try telling Alyssa that."

With a quick salute, he slides off the desk, gathers his belongings, and heads for the door. Then he pauses. "One more thing," he says in a serious voice. "You might want to avoid Principal Mahoney for a while. After your meeting yesterday, he seems to think that you and Ruben are like criminal

masterminds, hatching despicable plans behind his back."
He busts out laughing, and I laugh too, to show what a crazy
idea it is.

I don't mention that it also happens to be true.

BUILDING THE PERFECT CRIB

Mom picks me up from school and lugs me into the minivan. As usual, we've got an hour and a half to kill before PT, and today there's something I need to do.

"Mom," I say, "could you take me to Dee-Dub's house, please?"

She eyes me in the rearview mirror. "Dee-Dub?"

"Yeah. You know . . . Big kid. Math genius. Buys hair gel in bulk."

I don't think she was unclear on his identity. It's the other stuff that worries her: loose cannon . . . fondness for breaking noses.

"He's my friend," I remind her. "Plus, he went after Logan, which is almost like a public service."

Okay, that might be too much for Mom, who believes that a child's facial features should remain precisely where God intended. So I play my trump card: "Mr. Kostas told me to give him these math work sheets." I rummage in the backpack at my feet and pull them out. "I don't want him to get into trouble again."

Mom won't argue over schoolwork. Which is why she does a U-turn and drives in the direction of Dee-Dub's house.

Ten minutes later, we're sitting outside, the engine is idling, and I feel strangely nervous.

"I'd like to come in with you," she says.

By the time we make it to the front door, Mrs. Hardesty is waiting.

"Noah! Come on in." She calls Dee-Dub to come help me. The next thing I know, he's hoisting the back of my wheelchair over the step.

"Thanks," I say.

"Uh-huh," he replies, which isn't the same as "Hi" or "Good to see you" or "Thanks for coming around," but it's not the silent treatment either.

As Mom heads to the kitchen with Mrs. Hardesty, Dee-Dub

leads me to his computer station. It looks like he's spending his suspension from school playing Minecraft. I don't think that's the punishment Principal Mahoney had in mind when he sent Dee-Dub home yesterday.

"I've got work sheets for you from Mr. Kostas," I say. I place them beside the keyboard. "Sounds like you won't be coming back to school tomorrow."

He hangs his head the way Flub does whenever he whizzes on the kitchen floor. "My parents think I should take a break this week. Just in case."

"In case you break Logan's nose again?"

"Maybe."

"Oh. Well, don't. It's not worth it. Logan's nose is stuffed full of boogers. Trust me, you don't want his cooties getting on you."

Dee-Dub's eyes widen. "That's a good point. I really don't enjoy other people's boogers."

I'm about to ask him if he enjoys his own but change my mind. There are some things even a friend doesn't need to know.

"I wish you'd told me everything about the accident," he says, taking a seat beside me. "I don't like not knowing stuff."

"And what about you, huh? You never told me you're a

professional wrestler. Or that, you know, you've changed schools a lot."

He looks hurt. "Not a *lot*, but some. Mostly when I was younger. I'm better now."

"You could've fooled me."

It's a snarky thing to say and probably not very smart. Dee-Dub raises an eyebrow, but he doesn't get angry. I think that counts as progress.

"When we got to St. Louis, my parents said no one at school would know anything about me," he explains. "They said I'd be starting over. And it all worked out for a while. But I guess everyone knows me now."

"Oh, *please*! It was one fight. Plus, it was with Logan, so you were doing us all a favor. I'm going to start a petition, see if we can get the school to put up a statue of you."

Dee-Dub laughs, which is good to hear. Then the laughter dies out, and he's serious again. "Why do you like me, Noah?"

No one's ever asked me that question before. It feels awkward, like being asked for a Kleenex while your neighbor sobs in class. But if Dee-Dub's being honest with me, I should probably be honest with him too.

"Same reason you like me," I say. "Because you only see me like I am now. Everyone else at school remembers what I was like before the accident. Some of them even visited me in the hospital, but they didn't know what to say. It got so weird, I asked Mom not to let them in."

"Except Alyssa."

"Well, yeah. She's different."

"She's a girl, you mean."

"No. I mean, yeah! But that's not . . ." I shift my weight on the chair. The air conditioning is on, but I'm feeling a little warm. "We're just friends."

"That's what Gabriella Masterson always says too, right before she starts kissing boys."

My mouth hangs open. "Gabriella Masterson? That girl in the books? The one who goes around rescuing polar bears and sucking face all the time?"

"So you've read them too!" He wrinkles his nose, thinking. "What if Alyssa likes them as well? It could be a sign."

I mash a couple keys to wake up his computer. Anything to change the subject. As the monitor blinks to life, the image on it looks familiar: Busch Stadium—although Dee-Dub's been making improvements.

He clears his throat. "What actually happened the day of your accident, Noah?"

I tense up. Didn't I just tell him I liked having one person who didn't know about the accident? Why would he cross that line?

But just as suddenly, a strange calm comes over me. Dee-Dub's crossing that line for the same reason I want to know all about him, including his life in Albuquerque. Because it's a part of him, for better and for worse. How can we be friends if we don't really know each other?

"I was going to baseball when it happened," I begin. "Dad had been getting calls from work all morning because there was a problem with the store's computer system. But when Coach Montgomery told us there was going to be an extra practice, Dad dropped everything to take me.

"He was on another work call when his battery died. So he asked to borrow my phone instead. But I hadn't had a chance to talk with him all morning, and I wanted him to focus on us, you know?"

Dee-Dub doesn't answer. He knows it isn't a real question.

"Dad got annoyed when I didn't give him my phone. He said he didn't even know there was going to be practice, but he was giving me a ride anyway. I felt guilty, so I handed it over. But I wouldn't help him type the number for the store. That's why he was looking at the screen. He didn't look up until I screamed."

When I close my eyes, I can picture every terrifying detail of that moment. The car drifting in front of us. The sound of my voice. The jolt as Dad jams the brakes, locking the wheels. The hush as the car spins out of control. The bone-crushing crunch as we collide with the concrete underpass, and the smash of shattering glass. I can still smell the rubber we left smeared across the road.

"You must hate him," says Dee-Dub.

I open my eyes. "What?"

"Your dad . . . for what he did."

"It was an accident. If I'd just typed the number for him—"

"But he never should've been on the phone in the first place. There are statistics—it's as bad as driving drunk."

"He *died*."

"I know. And you could've died too. And it wasn't your fault."

I take a deep breath and remind myself that Dee-Dub isn't trying to be cruel. "I don't care whose fault it was. Dad's gone, and now everyone wants me to move on. But I don't want to move on. And I don't want Mom to move on either, especially not if it means hanging out with Mr. Dillon all the time."

"*All* the time?"

"Okay, maybe not. But definitely too much time."

I mean for this to end the conversation, but Dee-Dub doesn't notice. "How do you calculate that?" he asks.

"*Calculate* it?"

"Yeah." I can see the wheels turning in his brain. "There ought to be an algorithm. Something like: duration of relationship multiplied by a happiness coefficient. Wait, no! That wouldn't work. My parents say their honeymoon was the best week of their lives, and they'd only been together for six months."

"Uh, Dee-Dub . . . did you really just say 'happiness coefficient'?"

"Yeah." He chews on a fingernail. "That's what we need: a quantitative measurement of how happy they seem to be together, but with the objective factor of whether they *choose* to spend time together or apart when the opportunity is present."

I've always wanted to step into the world of Minecraft—my own parallel universe. Now I'm not so sure. Dee-Dub seems to spend most of his life stuck in a parallel universe, and it's a pretty strange place.

"Look at my parents," he says. "I'd say they rate almost ninety percent on the happiness meter. But once a week, Dad goes off to play poker with his friends instead of hanging out with Mom. Then again, he always wins, so he could argue that it's an extension of his work."

"Hey, Dee-Dub?"

He looks at me like he's forgotten I'm in the room. "Yeah?"

"What are you talking about?"

He nods. "Ah, I see. You're saying the algorithm needs refining. You're right—it's too simple at the moment."

A minute ago, I was fighting tears. Now I'm trying not to laugh. "Yup," I agree. "Way too simple. You need a lot more variables."

Stumped, Dee-Dub turns his attention to the computer monitor. The baseball diamond at Busch Stadium is complete now, and gigantic lights loom overhead. In the distance, the arch rises above the bleacher seating. The only thing that's out of place is the tower built behind home plate.

"What's that?" I ask.

"That's our crib."

"Our *crib*? Do people even use that word anymore?"

"I do," says Dee-Dub.

That's not exactly what I meant.

"Yeah," he continues. "I figured that since you're such a big baseball fan, you'd want a house on top of the stadium. I've seen the blueprints, remember, so I'm pretty sure the foundations are strong enough to support it."

I always dreamed that one day I'd get to play at Busch Stadium. Now I have a house there. Who knew?

"I thought this would help us visualize Operation GMU," he says. "Friday's game is only three days away."

"Your parents are still going to let you come?"

He nods energetically. "I promised them I'd behave."

"I'm not sure that unmasking Fredbird in the middle of a Cardinals game counts as behaving," I say.

"Can you think of another way to prove that Mr. Dillon isn't Fredbird?"

"No," I admit. "I can't."

"And his daughter needs to know the truth, right?

I almost say yes, but then I wonder, *Does she?* Makayla will be crushed when she discovers that the man inside the Fredbird suit isn't her dad. How can I ruin their relationship while I'm busy trying to patch things up between Mr. Riggieri and his kids?

"Listen, Dee-Dub," I say, stalling. "Operation GMU is amazing—"

"I know," he says.

"Right. And you've worked hard on it."

"Extremely hard," he agrees.

"Yeah. But I'm just not ready, you know?"

"I understand. You've been busy. That's why I took over the planning myself." He opens a drawer in his computer desk and pulls out a padded envelope. "Look," he says, emptying it, "here's the packet of itching powder, and here's a copy of the stadium blueprints so I can navigate to Fredbird's nest with maximum efficiency. I printed it out and folded it to fit precisely in the back pocket of my favorite pair of chinos."

"Uh . . ."

"So you see, Noah, I have everything under control."

It's true. He really does have everything under control. And he looks much happier with a project to focus on. Surviving middle school might be a stretch for Dee-Dub, but put him in charge of an honest-to-goodness criminal enterprise, and he makes it look easy.

"I'm still not sure about the operational code name, though," he says. "GMU just isn't right."

The code name is the last thing I'm worried about. I'm about to tell him so when our moms appear in the doorway.

"We need to get to PT, Noah," my mom says. "Don't want to be late."

For once, I actually agree with her.

As I turn the chair around, I take a final look at our crib on

241

the top of Busch Stadium. It's enormous, with tall windows and a deck as wide as twenty rows of bleacher seats.

"It's a sweet crib," I say.

"Nothing but the best for us," says Dee-Dub.

I can't help it: I start laughing. Seeing me, Dee-Dub laughs too.

"You're a funny dude, Dee-Dub."

"I guess I am," he says.

"And, uh, kind of unique."

He gives me a thumbs-up. "You too, Noah. You too."

DEALING WITH DYNAMO

Because of the detention, Mom has to move my PT session to Tuesday again. Somehow, Dynamo has moved his as well. In the past, this would've been my worst nightmare. Today, it's a bonus.

"Check this out, Angelica," I say, wiggling my left foot. Okay, *wiggle* is an exaggeration—it probably rises about half an inch, but that's half an inch more than last week.

Angelica stares at me, open-mouthed. It's not a good look for her, but I can tell she's impressed. "This is *progress!*" she exclaims.

The other PTs turn their heads to see what all the

excitement is about. Once I'm sure that Dynamo is watching too, I give another performance. I don't think he likes me being the center of attention, especially not when he's working his butt off on the clinic's climbing wall.

"That's it?" he calls down to me. "You're not even walking yet?"

He's pooping on my parade. I shouldn't let him get to me, but I'd really like to wipe that stupid, smug grin off his face.

"Sure," I say. "I'll walk."

Dynamo isn't expecting this. Even Angelica looks concerned. She shouldn't be, though. Last month, she told me there was no reason why I couldn't get on the treadmill like Dynamo.

"Let's do it," I say. "Strap me in."

"Me too," says Dynamo defiantly.

While Dynamo's PT helps him get down from the wall, Angelica straps me into a harness on a contraption called a LiteGait. She wheels it around so that I'm standing over the treadmill, and she starts the rubber belt. It's moving at a snail's pace, but the sensation is still very weird. I'm aware that my legs are moving, but I can't exactly feel them. Even when she manipulates my legs, helping me take my first steps, I'm not really in control. It reminds me of how I felt lying in the dust at Berra Park. I never want to feel that way again.

Once Dynamo is in his harness, he starts walking on a treadmill too.

"Faster," I say.

"Take it easy, champ," Angelica warns me. "Let's see how we do at this speed first."

"Faster," says Dynamo. "This is too easy."

Our treadmills are side by side, so I can see the display on his machine just as clearly as my own. We're going the same tragically slow speed, and Dynamo isn't happy about it.

"Just a little faster," he says.

His PT narrows her eyes but nudges the speed up a pip. He's now outpacing me by a blistering 0.1 miles per hour.

"More," he wheezes.

She takes him up again. Now he's racing away from me at 0.2 miles per hour. Okay, so he's not actually racing away because we're on treadmills, but he's still going faster, and he knows it.

"Put me up point two," I tell Angelica. "This is too easy."

That last part is a lie. I'm breathing heavily and sweating. It shouldn't be difficult to lope along at the same speed as a three-legged tortoise, but it is. Actually, it's exhausting.

Angelica matches my speed with Dynamo's. "No faster," she scolds. "This is *not* a competition."

I glance at Dynamo. Dynamo glances at me. The heck this isn't a competition—it's all-out war, and I have every intention of breaking Dynamo's legendary spirit.

We go shoulder to shoulder for ten seconds. Twenty seconds. Our PTs raise and lower our legs, making sure we make good contact with the treadmill belt. I'm not supporting my own body weight, and I'm not even taking steps independently, but the exercise is starting to take a toll. My pulse hasn't raced this fast in months. I imagine my chest bursting open and blood splattering against the mirrored walls, like in some kind of horror movie.

Dynamo is suffering too. His head is lolling about, and he's sucking air like a fish stranded on a beach. He wants to win, to show me he's still the boss, but he's hurting even more than I am. If I'm lucky, maybe his heart will splatter first. That would count as a win for me, right?

We soldier on for another ten seconds. Twenty. Thirty. Then Dynamo shakes his head, and his PT winds the treadmill down.

He's giving in. Surrendering. Waving the white flag.

I've won. I've actually *won*!

Angelica slows my treadmill down too, but now I feel like I could go on forever. Beating Dynamo has given me a jolt of energy. This must be what it feels like to win the World Series.

"Are you all right, Dynamo?" his PT asks.

Eyes closed, he nods. "You got tired of being my mascot, huh, Noah?"

"Something like that," I say. I could add that his *mascot* just destroyed him, but he's still struggling to catch his breath. My victory is already losing some of its shine.

Our PTs step away, leaving us to talk in private. I don't really want to talk to him, but now we're just dangling in our harnesses. If someone doesn't help us out, we could be stuck in these things forever, which reminds me how far I still have to go. Beating Dynamo doesn't change that.

"We're going to do this again next week," he says. "And next time, I won't wear myself out on the climbing wall."

I roll my eyes. "That's your excuse? You were tired?"

"It's not an excuse. It's true. I even did five minutes on the stairs before you got here," he says, pointing to a small set of wooden steps tucked into a corner of the room.

"You're a sore loser."

"The Dynamo wasn't born to lose."

That's the final straw. "Clearly you *were* born to lose because I just beat you—on my first try. You've been doing that treadmill for months too, so you had an unfair advantage."

"Unfair?" He sounds amused.

"Sure. Why not?"

He laughs but stops suddenly and winces like he's pulled a muscle. "None of this is fair," he says, grabbing his side. "I used to ride my bike every day. A year ago, this guy in a truck ran a red light. Hit me full on. Next thing I know, I wake up in the hospital and I can't feel anything."

I don't want to let Dynamo win this argument. I want him to admit that I beat him, fair and square. But I can already see my mistake. If there's a winner here, it's the kid who's been coming to physical therapy twice as long as I have and never complains. How does he stay so positive week after week? More important, why *isn't* he doing better?

Like he's reading my mind, Dynamo continues. "You want to know what else isn't fair? That you're an L. Probably L3, right? Or is it L4?"

This shuts me up real quick. L4 is medical jargon for a vertebra—a piece of bone in my spinal column. L stands for "lumbar," the level of the nerves that got damaged when this particular vertebra got shoved somewhere it shouldn't go. But there are thirty-three bones in the human spine, so how the heck did Dynamo guess?

"You're surprised, huh?" he says. "Well, don't be. I've been learning about the spine for a year. That's how I know I'll never be able to do the stuff you can do. If life was *fair*, I'd be L3 instead of T12." His eyes are welling up. "Three bones' difference—that's all it is. On my spine, that's, like, nothing. A freaking inch or two, and it means you'll get stronger and faster than me every single week."

I look away. Not just because Dynamo's on the verge of tears but because I am too. He's a nine-year-old kid. He was only eight when his accident happened. He never even got the chance to play on a Little League team. And he never will.

"We don't have to compete," I say quietly. "We could just . . . support each other."

Dynamo looks at me the way Mom looks at Flub when he makes a special delivery in the middle of the kitchen floor. "*Support* each other?" he mutters.

"Yeah. You know . . . cheer and stuff."

I think I've just made things worse.

"Just 'cause I can't beat you doesn't mean I can't win," he says. "Winning just means something different, that's all."

He shrugs. "My mom says we're all running our own races, anyway. The main thing is you've got to compete. Can't win anything without competing."

Angelica and the other PTs rejoin us. I don't know if they set Dynamo up to do this, and I guess it doesn't matter. He's been right about everything. I'm ashamed for not seeing it until now.

I reach out to pat him on the back, but he turns his head suddenly. "You're not about to get all mushy, are you?" he snaps.

"Huh? No!"

"Good." He holds out his fist, and we bump instead. "See you next week, then. Oh, and Noah?"

"Yeah?"

"You need a new nickname. Mascot doesn't cut it anymore."

EVEN CRAZY KIDS SOMETIMES MAKE SENSE

On Thursday, Mrs. Friendly has the class running in circles again. She says something about "concussion protocol" to Alyssa, but Alyssa refuses to sit out, so the two of us drift around the gym in super slow motion. Our classmates lap us every thirty seconds.

"Did you really have to go to the hospital?" I ask her.

"Yeah. Just so they could check me out." She leans over and parts her hair. "I've got an awesome goose egg." She points at the angry red welt on her scalp.

Instinctively, I reach up and touch it. But as soon as I

feel her hair and skin, I freeze up. Alyssa doesn't pull away, though, or tell me to stop. Does that mean she's okay with it?

"You two back together again or what?" drones Logan, jogging past us.

I slide my fingers away from her head as Alyssa straightens. Both of us are blushing as we resume our tour of the gym.

"I can't believe Principal Mahoney let him back already," I say.

"No kidding."

"I'll tell Dee-Dub to hit him harder next time."

"No you won't, Noah Savino." Alyssa bats my arm. "And you shouldn't joke about it."

Heavy footsteps drum behind us as Logan catches up again. His left knee must have finally healed. Too bad his nose is swollen like a parakeet's bill. He slows down to match our pace and trails us like a pesky shadow. "So, when's the wedding?" he asks.

"Grow up, Logan," says Alyssa.

"Fine. You want to keep it under wraps. I get it." He leans toward me. "When's the baseball rematch, though?"

"You've got to be kidding," I say.

"No. I saw you both practicing with Monster Truck at Berra Park, remember?"

"That was before you got him *suspended*!"

"Oh, yeah." He wipes the back of his hand across his tender nose and makes an odd whimpering sound, like a distressed bunny. "But I covered for him, right? I didn't tell Mahoney that he started it. I almost took the blame myself."

"Because you *were* to blame," I say. "You were a complete jerk, just like always."

"Oh, come on. I was just kidding around."

I stop my chair suddenly, and Logan crashes into me. He hits the floor hard, and I almost topple over too. In a heartbeat, Alyssa is standing over him, looking as wild as Dee-Dub when he rearranged Logan's face.

"How do you have any friends left?" she snarls. "Seriously. The way you treat people . . ."

Heaving himself off the wooden floor, Logan narrows his eyes. "What about it?"

"You're horrible! Noah could've died in that car accident, and you keep making fun of him. Who does that?"

"Just trying to keep it real," says Logan defensively.

Other students are tuning in to the standoff, which is kind

of embarrassing. I'd like to speak for myself, but Alyssa's way too angry to stop now.

"Keep it *real*?" she exclaims.

Logan grits his teeth. "Well, what about you, huh? You boss him around, and he doesn't even notice. He sure as heck doesn't shut you out. No one shuts *you* out."

"What are you talking about?" I ask.

"You know exactly what I'm talking about. I visited you twice in the hospital. *Twice!* The first time, your mom said you weren't ready for visitors, which was a total lie 'cause Alyssa said she already saw you. A week later, it was Little Miss Perfect here who told me to get lost."

"I never said that!" protests Alyssa.

"You said Noah didn't want to see me. Same difference. And don't pretend you didn't enjoy telling me to go away."

Alyssa is turning a bright shade of red. I'm pretty sure I am too. I don't understand why I'm suddenly feeling defensive, but Mrs. Friendly is keeping out of the argument, which makes me think our good-versus-evil standoff isn't as clear-cut as it was a few moments ago.

"Tell me I'm wrong," Logan says, looking at me now, not Alyssa.

"What did you expect?" I say. "We were never friends,

Logan. And there I was, lying in bed, thinking about how I'd never play baseball again, and . . ." My voice is rising, and I don't want to cry. So I swallow my thoughts and look away.

Logan is silent for a few seconds. "But *I* wanted to see *you*," he says.

"Why? So you could gloat? Or pretend like you cared?"

Head bowed, Logan scans the gym and the dozens of pairs of eyes fixed on us. "No. So I could . . . say sorry."

Sorry. That word, and the stillness that comes after it, is like the calm that follows a summer thunderstorm. But I still don't understand what's going on.

"Sorry for *what*?" I ask.

"For everything. For being mean to you. For chewing you out every time we lost a game. For my dad calling an extra practice the day you had the accident." He picks at his thumbnail. "We all figured you were just late, you know? But my mom heard the news from one of your neighbors, and she called my dad, and he made us huddle, and he told us what happened. He said your dad died and you wouldn't be catching for us anymore . . . maybe ever again. Like, *never.*"

From the corner of his eye, Logan must be able to see how everyone is listening. This is his chance to stand tall, flash us his best Draco Malfoy sneer, and walk away. But he doesn't.

"We all started crying when Coach . . . my dad . . . told us," he continues. "He made us snap out of it. Said you were injured, not dead, and you're still Noah, so we should treat you the same as always. But I couldn't. So I bought a card and got all the team to sign it, and I brought it to the hospital. Left it with your mom when she said I couldn't see you."

I remember the card well. It was huge, for one thing, but it was more about the messages inside—the rest of the team telling me I was going to pull through, and they believed in me, and how much I inspired them. I remember reading it all and feeling even more lost than before. They didn't know the first thing about my injuries, and they didn't really even know *me*. Why did I *inspire* them? It didn't make sense.

"I didn't know the card was from you," I say.

He shrugs. "Doesn't matter. Point is, I wanted us to start over. I wanted to be different than I was before. But you wouldn't let me. You wouldn't even *see* me. So when school started, I figured instead of acting all weird around you like everyone else, I'd just be like I always was."

He lets his arms fall to his sides. Alyssa and I exchange glances.

"Let me get this straight," she says. "You're a jerk to Noah because you've *always* been a jerk?"

He takes a moment to think this over, probably because he realizes how bad it sounds. "Well . . . yeah. Look," he says, appealing to me, "just because I was the best pitcher and you were the best catcher doesn't mean we actually liked each other. I get that. We made it work because we wanted to win, that's all. So, be honest, how would you feel if I suddenly started being all nice to you just 'cause you're in a wheel-chair?"

Alyssa huffs. Yet again, Logan is dazzling us with his talent for being offensive. The weird thing is, I'm not offended.

For once, Logan is actually making sense. The only thing we ever had in common was a drive to be the best ballplayers we could be. Yes, he was a bully, and I hated that about him. But he hated that, as catcher, I got to call the pitches. Just like he hated that it was my call to let him into my hospital room . . . or to turn him away.

I don't know if I truly hate Logan anymore, but I can't think of a reason to like him either. We didn't get along as teammates. Why should we get along when the only thing that connected us has gone?

Mrs. Friendly blows her whistle. "You three planning on joining us today?" she yells.

We're the only ones who haven't finished the circuit. Alyssa, embarrassed, takes off jogging, but Logan stays beside me as I roll slowly around the gym.

"I've been wanting to tell you about my dad," he says, scratching his armpit.

"Coach? What about him?"

"He's been different since your accident. Like, at practices he doesn't chew me out in front of everyone. Sometimes, he even says I did good."

"Sounds like a miracle," I say.

"Yeah. It kind of feels like one too." He shoots me a lopsided grin. "The team didn't do so good once he went soft on us, but we all like each other more."

"You can be lovable losers."

"Sure. And you can be our mascot."

I look up sharply, but he's already stifling a laugh. "Sorry," he says. "Just had to get in one more dig."

"Hmm." I push the wheels a little harder so that he has to speed up. "My mascot days are over."

"Yeah. I think they are too. Now I think you want to beat me at baseball."

"Alyssa's pitching, not me."

"Yeah. But you'll be calling the pitches. Plus, I watched you working with her and the big kid." He touches his nose gently like he wants to make sure it's still there. "Admit it, you'd do anything to beat me."

I can't deny it. I miss our Little League team. I miss baseball. Which is why I need to finish what Alyssa started on the school blacktop a couple weeks ago. Because Alyssa and Dee-Dub and I are a team now, and I want us to win more than ever.

"Saturday morning," I tell him. "Ten o'clock at Berra Park. Don't be late."

"I won't. You can count on it."

As we rejoin our class, Logan holds out his fist for me to bump. We used to do it every time he pitched another amazing game. It was his way of admitting that he couldn't do it alone. That great pitching is a team effort.

For the first time in months, I bump his fist right back, and he smiles like he knows exactly what I'm thinking.

Game on!

Alyssa spends the rest of PE giving me strange looks. Half an hour later, as forty sweaty bodies file out of the gym, she corners me. "Don't tell me we're actually going through with this crazy pitch-off," she says.

"Okay. I won't tell you."

She purses her lips. "Seriously? Logan insults you every chance he gets, and you still want to play ball with him."

"Not *with* him. Against him."

"And what about Dee-Dub? How do you think he's going to feel?"

"I think he's going to feel great when he hits Logan's pitch out of the park."

Alyssa grabs her gym bag. "You're not going to cheat, are you?"

I pretend to gasp but accidentally swallow my spit and end up coughing instead. "That's a . . . terrible thing . . . to say," I wheeze.

She flicks her head toward the hallway, and I follow her out of the gym.

"So, when's this happening?" she asks.

"Saturday morning."

"But that's when we're with Mr. Riggieri."

"Sure is."

She skips in front of my wheelchair and plants her hands on the arms, jolting me to a stop. "Okay. Spit it out. What's going on?"

"What do you mean?"

"I can read you like a book, Noah Savino. You've got

something up your sleeve. More than just the pitch-off. What is it?"

"I don't know what you're talking about."

"Whatever." She blows her bangs out of her eyes. "Saturday morning wasn't looking good for me anyway."

"Okay, fine!" I groan. "I found out that Mr. Riggieri and his kids don't talk anymore, so I came up with this plan to get them back together."

"Are you sure that's a good idea?"

"Trust me, the plan is perfect."

Alyssa frowns. It's not the response I was hoping for, but it's not exactly surprising either. Asking her to trust me with a secret plan is like asking Flub not to dig up a liver treat I just buried in the backyard

She lets go of my wheelchair arms and glances at her watch. "Come on," she says. "We're going to be late for class. Don't want to get in trouble."

"Trouble? Guess you haven't heard: I'm a bad boy now. Got my first detention on Monday."

Alyssa stares at me for a moment and then busts out laughing. "Getting detention from Principal Mahoney doesn't make you a rebel. Just means you must've been really, really stupid."

I bump my wheelchair gently against her legs, and she laughs even harder.

"Was that supposed to be rebellious too?" she asks. "I can't tell."

We join the main hallway, which is always busy. It's hard to glide along gracefully when my wheelchair covers several square feet of ground, but Alyssa stands tall and together we carve a channel through the traffic. When we branch off along a quieter hallway, she looks down at me again.

"I like it that you stand up to Logan now," she says.

"Eh, he's lucky I went easy on him."

Alyssa smiles, but she doesn't laugh. "Can I ask . . ." She bites her lip. "When I visited you in the hospital after the accident, why didn't you send me away too?"

If she'd asked me that question a month ago, I don't think I would've answered it. But things are different now. "Because you knew me better than anyone else. And I felt like I knew you better than anyone else too."

"Oh."

"Yeah. Also, you didn't make me think about baseball."

I figure she's going to ask me what she *did* make me think about, but instead she chuckles. "That's kind of ironic. Seeing as how we're a team now."

"True. Different kind of team, though."

"Different kind of Noah."

I fidget in my chair. "You mean, my legs . . ."

She tsks. "There's a lot more to you than your legs, Noah Savino."

The way she says it, her voice a little quieter and breathier than before, makes me feel kind of tingly. "You, uh, saying my legs are ugly?" I croak.

"I'm saying there're parts of you that are cuter. Parts I prefer to look at."

I check out my arms and chest.

"Your face, doofus!"

"Oh" I turn bright red, which will probably make her change her mind about my face.

Or maybe not. Because a moment later, she touches my arm, and suddenly it's the only part of me that matters.

REUNITING RIGGIERIS

The Hill is less than one square mile in area. I know this because I got Dad to look it up once. I must've been in first grade, and the neighborhood seemed huge to me. I couldn't imagine why anyone would ever need to leave.

When Dad told me how small it is, I was disappointed. So he pointed along our street to Yogi Berra's house and Joe Garagiola's house and told me the stories of where they started and how they rose to the top of the baseball world. And how they always made sure to come back home again.

"When you leave The Hill, you take a piece of it with you,"

he said. "So you could say we're at the heart of America, right here on this street."

That made sense to me then. But I'm older now, and I know how small one square mile is. Which is why I'm certain the only way Mr. Riggieri and his son can avoid bumping into each other is to make sure it never happens.

That stops today.

After I finish my homework, I sit at the computer and pull up the list of Riggieri family addresses I found a few days ago. Then I write them down on a scrap of paper. I'm so busy I don't hear Mom enter the room.

"That's a lot of Riggieris," she says.

Without thinking, I close the browser window. Then I wish I hadn't. Now she's going to think I'm up to no good.

"I'm sorry I told you that stuff about Mr. Riggieri the other day," she says. "He's always been polite to me. I wasn't trying to ruin things between you."

I turn my chair around. "I know, Mom."

"I just wanted you to see that no one is perfect. Not me. Not Mr. Riggieri . . . And maybe not Mr. Dillon. But Odell has put up with a lot the past year, and he's never stopped trying to help people. Remind you of someone?"

I nod.

"Yeah," she says. "And it's been nice for me to have someone to lean on the past couple weeks, but . . . I know it's been hard for you, seeing him around here. So I've asked him to stay away for now."

I can't believe it. Mr. Dillon is out of our lives, just like that. I feel like I should be celebrating or at least thanking Mom for cutting him loose. Instead, I've got this weird feeling in my gut.

"You know what's most amazing?" says Mom. "When I spoke to Odell, he was totally okay about everything. He made me promise only one thing."

"What's that?"

"That we'd still use the tickets for Friday's game. Isn't that something?"

Yes, it is. In fact, it's exactly the kind of thing Dad would've done.

Mom is smiling, but it doesn't look real. She seems empty . . . and lost. The way I'd probably feel if she told me that Dee-Dub is dangerous and she doesn't want me hanging out with him anymore.

Which is ironic, because at this very moment Dee-Dub is working on a risky plan to prove that Mr. Dillon's not

Fredbird. I'll definitely need to make it clear to him that Operation GMU is off now. He'll be disappointed, but he'll get over it.

"So, are you going to tell me why you were looking up Mr. Riggieri's family?" Mom asks.

I try to hide the scrap of paper in my hands, which just draws more attention to it. "It's . . . well, it's kind of a secret."

"A secret?" She looks worried.

"Trust me, it's a good thing."

"Trust you?" She snorts. "On the week you got your first detention?"

"I admit, the timing's not ideal."

She laughs at that. "God, you're so much like your dad," she says, tearing up. "He loved you like crazy   I love you like crazy."

She steps forward and hugs me tight against her. It feels strange at first—we haven't hugged like this in ages—but then I relax into her arms. We'll never be the same as we were before Dad died, but at least we've still got each other.

"I do trust you, Noah," she whispers into my hair. "You're a good kid, and I believe in you. So go on," she says, letting me go. "Do whatever it is you need to do. And make me proud."

I wheel outside and down the ramp. My chair and I cast a long shadow as I head along the street. Botanical is only a few hundred yards away, even closer than Berra Park, and in a few minutes, I'm staring up at a neat little house with blue painted walls and green trim. Marco Riggieri's yard is as tidy as his dad's.

Unfortunately, I am definitely looking *up* at his house, and I don't see any way to get to the door.

There's a newspaper in a blue plastic bag at the edge of his property. If I throw it at his front door, I might be able to get his attention. So I pick it up, take aim, and imagine that I'm Alyssa Choo, pitcher extraordinaire.

Unfortunately, thinking of Alyssa reminds me of the pitches that ended up in Dee-Dub's gut. As I release the bag, I choke out an enormous laugh. Which is not very smart, because it means that (1) I don't notice the front door opening, and (2) Marco Riggieri's first impression is of me laughing at him as he takes a newspaper to the head.

"What the heck!" He narrows his eyes and shoots me a scary look that's right out of Mr. Riggieri's playbook. Like father, like son.

And they *are* alike. Marco is taller than his dad and even

more powerful looking, but otherwise, he looks exactly like I imagine Mr. Riggieri did about forty years ago, even down to the curly hair.

He thunders down his porch steps and strides toward me. Now would be a good moment for me to run off, but that would require my legs to work. So I just sit there like a statue as he comes to a stop in front of me, muscular arms folded across his broad chest.

"You hit me," he says.

This is not how I planned to start our conversation, but I definitely have his attention. "Uh, yes," I say. "But I've got a good reason."

Muttering, he spins on his heel and walks away.

"I'm here on a mission," I say.

"Uh-huh!" he shouts over his shoulder.

"It's about your dad."

Marco stops walking. Turns slowly and watches me again. He doesn't look angry like he did before, but somehow his expression is even more menacing. "What's going on?"

I should be scared, but I'm not. I can't even explain why. I just know that if I'm being as honest as Alyssa and as direct as Dee-Dub, I must be doing the right thing. (Well, apart from whacking Marco on the noggin with a newspaper. That was admittedly a mistake.)

"Your dad . . . Mr. Riggieri . . . ," I begin. "He's been coaching me and my friends in baseball. Ten o'clock, every Saturday morning."

Marco doesn't say anything. He still looks annoyed. Actually, he looks like he could probably disconnect my arms, lay me out with a Dee-Dub hammer blow, and not break a sweat.

"Yeah, so . . . ," I continue, a little less confidently, "he's been coaching us, right? And I got to talking with him about how you two don't talk anymore, and I thought . . . well, I thought maybe you could start talking again."

Okay, so I clearly should've spent a little less time doing research on the Riggieri family and a little more time planning what I was actually going to say.

"Did my father send you?" he asks.

"No."

"Did he tell you all the things he said to me?"

"Not exactly, no."

"No," repeats Marco, like this closes the case. "Look, I don't know what your dad is like, but mine was a tyrant. There's a reason I stay away from him."

"My dad is dead," I say.

Marco stares at me. I didn't plan to tell him about Dad—it just popped out—but isn't this really the difference between us? Not that my dad was amazing and his was awful. But that he and Mr. Riggieri still have a chance at a future together.

He places his hands on his hips. "Are you the kid that lives across the street from him?"

"Yeah."

"Noah, right? Noah Savino?"

"The one and only," I say, trying hopelessly to smile.

Marco takes a seat on a porch step and rests his elbows on his knees. "I remember when you were a baby. Most of the time, I saw you with your mom, and she'd be singing or telling you the names of everything. But sometimes your dad was pushing the stroller. You'd be all decked out in Cardinals gear and mouthing on an old leather catcher's mitt. That glove sure seemed to keep you happy."

"I've still got it," I tell him.

"You don't still chew on it, though, right?"

"Not as much as I used to."

He laughs, and suddenly I can see the warmer, kinder side of Mr. Riggieri Senior shining through.

Behind him, the front door opens and another man walks out. The new guy isn't as big and intimidating as Marco. "So, this is where you got to," he says.

Without looking around, Marco raises a hand. "Phil, this is my old neighbor, Noah Savino. Noah, this is Phil."

"Good to meet you, Noah," says Phil.

"You too," I say.

"Noah here's been getting baseball coaching from my father," Marco explains.

Phil sucks in air through his teeth. "Yikes. Good luck with that."

"I think he wants me to come watch on Saturday," continues Marco. "Isn't that right, Noah? So I can see what a stand-up guy my father has become."

I don't like his tone. It's like he's making a joke that I can't understand.

"Yes," I say.

Phil takes a seat on the porch steps too but a couple up from Marco. "I think we should go along."

Marco stiffens. "Don't you remember what he said to us? To *you*?"

"Of course I do," says Phil. "Every word. But I also remember him standing right where Noah is now and saying he was sorry."

When Marco doesn't respond, Phil places a hand on his

shoulder and squeezes once. That's when it hits me. I don't think Marco and his father fell out over baseball. I think they fell out because of Phil.

Marco, hunched over, is quiet now. I want to tell him more about how his father has changed, but I think he already knows. The question is whether that's enough to undo the past.

"Saturday," I remind him. "Ten o'clock. Berra Park."

Then, turning my wheelchair, I begin the short journey home.

OPERATION GMU

On Friday evening, we pick up Dee-Dub on our way to the Cardinals game. While Mom chats with his parents, he climbs into the front passenger seat. I'm stuck in the back with Makayla, so it's difficult to tell him that Operation GMU is officially over. If he'd been at school today I would've told him, but he was still on suspension for his last bad idea.

"You ready, Noah?" Dee-Dub calls back from the front seat.

"Yes," I say. "Should be a great game."

"I'm not talking about the game." He tries to turn around in his seat, but he's kind of wedged in. "I'm talking about Operation GMU."

"What's Operation GMU?" Makayla asks.

"Nothing," I say, getting flustered. "It's just a thing between Dee-Dub and me."

"That's right," agrees Dee-Dub. "Just you and me and Alyssa."

My stomach plummets like I'm free-falling on a roller coaster. "What's Alyssa got to do with it?"

His shoulders bob up and down. "She came to my house this afternoon. She said you told her you were working on a secret plan, but she wasn't clear on the details. So I filled her in."

"You *what*? That was a different plan!"

"Are you saying you've got a backup plan?" Dee-Dub sounds confused. "You think Operation MUD won't work?"

"A moment ago, you called it Operation *GMU*," says Makayla, flicking her hair beads like she means business.

"Same difference," explains Dee-Dub. "Although I still think MUD works better. It stands for—"

"Mud!" I shout. "It stands for mud! Anyway, my *other* plan

isn't a backup for anything. It's called Operation Reunite Riggieri."

"Like our *neighbor* Riggieri?" says Makayla.

Oh, shoot. I forgot that she knows him too. "Uh . . ."

"You're not planning to unmask Mr. Riggieri as well, are you?" exclaims Dee-Dub.

"Who else are you unmasking?" cries Makayla. "Is that the GMU-MUD thing you keep talking about?"

"No!" I say.

"Yes!" says Dee-Dub.

Makayla is giving me the evil eye. As if that's not bad enough, Alyssa knows our secret too. Together, they could make it very difficult for me to cover everything up.

"Your dad said tonight's game is sold out, right?" I ask Makayla.

"Yeah," she says. "Why?"

"No reason." I relax into my seat.

One adversary is better than two.

We arrive early and park the car. Ten minutes later, I'm wheeling toward Busch Stadium. We're only twenty yards away from the third base entrance when Dee-Dub stops.

"Is that Alyssa?" he asks.

I whip my head around. It's Alyssa all right. She's standing near the ticket booths about fifty yards away, and I can guess why she's here.

I can't let her see us. If she comes over and starts talking about Operation GMU in front of Mom, we'll be in big trouble. It won't even matter that I'm trying to call the whole thing off.

"Let's go," I say.

I'm almost at the gate when Alyssa turns around. At first, she furrows her brows like she vaguely remembers seeing me before. Then she narrows her eyes. I feel like we're in a Wild West standoff, waiting to see who blinks first.

Turns out, it's me. The moment I put my hands on the wheels, she starts sprinting toward us. Lucky for me, Mom's already handing our tickets to the attendant.

"I need to pee!" I shout.

I've said the magic words. The attendant hustles us through, and we barrel along the concourse. Twenty seconds later, we're safe, and I'm sweating.

"Restroom's over there," says Mom, breathing heavily.

"False alarm," I tell her.

Mom isn't very happy, but she doesn't complain—it has taken me months to get some control over my lower regions, and she's not going to make me feel bad about it now.

Mom leads us the short distance to Section 160, where Mr. Dillon is already waiting for us. He gives her a brief hug, which reminds me why we came up with Operation GMU in the first place. "This way," he says, pointing to a passageway.

"I'll wait here," says Makayla, leaning against the wall.

"Sure thing, honey." Mr. Dillon turns to Mom and whispers, "She's waiting for you-know-who."

Mom smiles. "Ah, young love."

"Heaven help us all," replies Mr. Dillon, sighing.

You-know-who? Young love? Before I can ask what they're talking about, Mr. Dillon leads us into the passageway. A few seconds later, we emerge to an ocean of bright red seats and grass trimmed so flat it looks like carpet. In the distance, the Gateway Arch is bathed in yellow light from the setting sun. It's beautiful.

I've been to Busch Stadium before but always with Dad. Seeing it reminds me of those times—how I'd bring Dad's old catcher's mitt in case a fly ball made it to our section, although it never did. I wish I'd remembered to bring the glove today.

Dad would've loved these seats. Well, not seats exactly—

more like an area for me to park my wheelchair and folding chairs for everyone else—but the view is fantastic. We're halfway between third base and home plate, close enough to see the catcher's signals, and the pitcher's windup, and the batter's grip. Close enough to feel like we're part of the game, not just watching it.

I don't know how much money a refuse consultant makes, but I'm pretty sure Mr. Dillon just spent a chunk of it trying to impress Mom and me.

Dee-Dub nudges me. He points to the large ring of keys clipped to Mr. Dillon's belt. He's clearly itching to get started on GMU, but I shake my head. There'll be time to explain to him why the operation is off. For now, I just want to enjoy the view.

"I should probably check on Makayla," says Mr. Dillon, peering back into the passageway.

"I'll come with you," says Mom brightly. "You two are okay here, right?" she asks Dee-Dub and me.

"Sure," I say. I don't even mind that Mom is going with Mr. Dillon. After all, he's going to have to leave us alone for the entire game to keep up the illusion that he's Fredbird. I almost feel sorry for him, buying these amazing seats and then missing all the action just to keep up one crazy lie.

"So," says Dee-Dub the moment they're gone. "About Operation MUD—"

"GMU," I correct him.

"Exactly, MUD. We're a go, right?"

Oh, boy. "Listen, Dee-Dub. I've been thinking. This whole operation doesn't feel right."

"It's perfect," he says, bouncing his leg up and down like a toddler who needs to go potty.

"I'm not saying it isn't brilliant. But remember the other night when you talked about too many variables? Operation GMU feels kind of like that."

"No, it doesn't."

Geez. I guess I'm going to need a different approach.

"I think Makayla's on to us," I say. "She heard you say 'GMU' . . . and 'MUD'!"

"So what? You said she needs to know the truth about her dad, remember? She'll probably thank us."

"Oh, for— The plan is off, Dee-Dub, okay? Think about it: we couldn't even get hold of Mr. Dillon's keys. And that was step one!"

"These keys?" he says, pulling a large ring from his pocket.

My stomach goes into free fall again. "Where did you get those?"

"From Mr. Dillon's belt."

"But . . . but that was going to be *my* job."

"You seemed preoccupied."

"I wasn't *preoccupied*. I was . . . ugh! We need to get those back to him, Dee-Dub!"

"But I only just stole them."

"Stole what?" demands Makayla, appearing behind us.

"Nothing," I say. Or begin to say, anyway. The word gets stuck in my throat on account of how Makayla's not alone, and the boy beside her is familiar. Horribly familiar, from his wheelchair to his toilet-brush Mohawk.

Freaking Dynamo!

"Well, look here," says Dynamo, raising a hand in greeting. "It's my old mascot."

I'm too confused to be angry. "H-How do you two know each other?"

"Makayla's my girlfriend," explains Dynamo. "You didn't believe me when I said I was dating, but hey, it's cool. You've got trust issues. I get it."

Makayla takes his hand and squeezes it, like they're an actual couple. They're *nine*, for Pete's sake. Why hasn't anyone told them that nine-year-old kids don't date? And where are our parents, anyway?

"Oooh, look!" exclaims Dynamo, pointing at the field. He waves his arm back and forth. I have no idea who he's waving at because the only person there is one of the Cardinals cheering squad.

The woman waves back at him. Then she *blows him a kiss*.

"Your sister's pretty," Makayla tells him.

"Uh-huh," replies Dynamo. "But don't tell Noah that. He doesn't believe my sister's a cheerleader."

Makayla purses her lips. "Wow, Noah. You really *do* have trust issues."

"But it sort of makes sense," Dynamo says. "You know, after the spelling bee thing."

"Oh, that was awesome," Makayla crows.

"I still can't believe you *changed the words*, Noah." Dynamo shakes his head. "Makayla figured she could set you up— get you to feed her pages to the dog or something. I told her, no way is anyone *that* stupid. But you . . ." He slaps his legs, laughing. "You went all the way. Like she wouldn't even notice!"

Dee-Dub gives me a sympathetic look, like he's watching a starting pitcher unravel on the mound. I want to defend myself, but (1) I'm not sure that's possible and (2) he still has the keys in his hand, and time is running out.

"I wonder where our parents are," I say loudly.

"They were talking in the passageway just now," says Makayla. "I think your mom's worried about you, Noah."

"No wonder," mutters Dynamo.

I'd like to fire back with something clever, but I can't think of anything, and anyway, I need Dee-Dub to return the keys.

"So," I say, catching Dee-Dub's eye. "My mom and *Mr. Dillon* are *in the passageway.*"

Dee-Dub watches me with a glazed expression. "That's what Makayla just said, yes."

Sheesh. If I can't get through to him with verbal hints, I might need to try another approach. I try staring at the keys in his balled-up fingers and then flick my head in the direction of the concourse, signaling that it's time for him to leave. When he doesn't move, I do it again, and this time I wink too.

"Oh," he says, jumping up so fast he almost topples over. "Yes. I'm, uh, going to the restroom."

Dee-Dub shuffles past us and dives into the passageway. I don't know how he's possibly going to explain to Mr. Dillon why he has the keys, but he's smart—I'm sure he'll figure something out.

Dynamo watches him go. "That's one huge dude. Is he the one who got suspended from your school?"

I shoot Makayla a nasty look.

"What?" she says. "Your mom told my dad. I didn't realize it was a secret."

Dynamo snorts. "You two are hilarious. You sound like you're brother and sister already."

"That's not funny," says Makayla.

"Neither was setting me up to ruin your spelling bee sheets," I remind her.

"How else was I supposed to get rid of you and your mom?"

I gasp. *"What?"*

Standing over me with her arms folded, Makayla reminds me a lot of Alyssa. "My dad and I were doing fine before you came along. Then Dad says he wants to hang out with your mom, and he got me this really boring babysitter. Then, two days later, he makes me hang out with you, and you're even worse. So I decided they needed to stop seeing each other. I did that whole "sucking face" thing in front of your mom, but it wasn't enough. So I got you to ruin my spelling bee, and it still didn't work. In the end, I just told him I didn't like him spending so much time with your mom."

"And what did he say?" I ask.

She shrugs. "He said he liked having someone to talk to.

But he also said he'd stop seeing her if it's what I wanted."

I don't believe it. After all this time, it turns out I could've just waited for Makayla to force our parents apart. It never occurred to me that she felt the same way I did, holding tight to her only parent because there's no one else.

"The thing is," she continues, "now that my dad's promised not to see your mom anymore, I wish I hadn't said anything. I'd prefer to be around two happy people than one unhappy one. You know what I mean?"

I nod. "Yeah. Actually, I do."

"Even you're not *so* bad, Noah. Like, my teacher told me how you came by and owned up to what you did." Makayla winds a string of hair beads around her finger. "The way I see it, only a good person would do that. Dynamo kind of likes you now too, and that's saying something, because he used to think you were a loser."

"Takes one to know one," I say.

"That's the best you got?" Dynamo sneers.

"You're so full of yourself."

"The Dynamo won't pretend to be any less brilliant than he is."

I glance at Makayla, and we both roll our eyes.

It's strange, but sharing this moment with her is like glimpsing a new and different version of the future. Sure, it'd involve seeing Mr. Dillon and Makayla again, but that doesn't seem as bad as it did just an hour ago.

It's just as well I went ahead and canceled Operation GMU. I can picture it now: Fredbird bounding onto the field wearing a mask filled with itching powder, then tearing it off as the crowd goes quiet. I imagine Mom and Makayla staring in horror as they discover that it's not Mr. Dillon in the suit after all. The whole thing gives me chills.

Dynamo rolls back a few feet and stares down the passageway. "Is your friend okay, Noah?" he asks. "I mean, I thought *we* had issues, but that dude's been gone for *ages*."

It's a good point, especially as Dee-Dub wasn't even going as far as the toilets. Maybe Mr. Dillon and Mom weren't at the end of the passageway, and he had to go look for them. Yeah, that must be it, because the only other explanation is that he went through with the plan after all, and he wouldn't do that until I gave him a sign. And since we hadn't actually agreed on a sign—

I feel the blood drain from my face. I winked at him just before he left. I *winked*, just like Alyssa winked on the school blacktop. Did Dee-Dub think *that* was the sign?

I spin my chair around and power back toward the con-course. Forget about calling things off. I think Operation GMU is happening *right now*.

DEE-DUB TO THE RESCUE

The concourse is flooded with Cardinals fans in red-and-white baseball shirts. I can hardly move. I don't know which way to go, anyway. Dee-Dub's got the stadium blueprints tucked in the pocket of his favorite chinos.

Why didn't I get a copy too?

As one half of a criminal mastermind team, I'm totally out of my league.

"Wait up!" shouts Makayla, jogging to catch up with me. Dynamo is rolling along behind her.

Great! Now there are going to be witnesses. At least

Makayla probably knows her way around the place.

"Where does Fredbird get dressed?" I ask.

Dynamo pulls a face. "Ew. Why do you want to watch Fredbird getting dressed?"

"I don't. I just need to know where he is."

"His nest is downstairs," says Makayla. "There's an elevator. But they won't let you on it."

"They'll let *me* on it," says Dynamo confidently. "*Everyone* knows the Dynamo." And just like that, he dives into the mass of Cardinals fans.

It takes us a minute to get to the elevator. A security guard is looking at me suspiciously, but then he sees Dynamo, and suddenly they're bumping fists and the doors are opening. I might be in time to catch Dee-Dub after all.

"Noah!" Alyssa sprints through the crowd and skids to a halt beside me. "You. Are. An. Idiot!"

I try to tell her with my eyes that she needs to calm down, but I guess Alyssa isn't very good at reading eyeball language.

"What are you *thinking*?" she snaps.

"I'm, uh, thinking that it'd be nice to take an elevator ride," I say, trying to sound more relaxed than I feel.

"Well, you know what I think? I think you and Dee-Dub need brain transplants. I think you should be locked up for your own safety. I . . . I . . ."

Dynamo pulls alongside me. "Is this your girlfriend?" he asks.

"No, I am *not* his girlfriend!" growls Alyssa. "I prefer boys with functioning brains."

Dynamo covers his mouth with his hand. "I think she likes you," he whispers.

"I do *not* like him," says Alyssa. "And neither would you if you knew what he's up to."

I pretend to have a coughing fit, which is so convincing that it actually leads to a real coughing fit. By the time I can breathe again, the elevator doors are about to close. The guard holds them open and I hurry on board.

"You should wait out there," I wheeze as Alyssa follows me.

"Not a chance," she mutters. "I didn't spend fifty bucks on a scalped ticket so you could make the biggest mistake of your life. And what about Dee-Dub? He's only just finished his suspension for beating up Logan."

"Wait. That big kid got suspended for *fighting*?" squeaks Dynamo. He glances at me. "Are you two, like, hit men?"

I could tell him to be quiet, but it's kind of fun to see

Dynamo looking worried.

"Listen, Alyssa," I say. "I'm trying to make sure that Dee-Dub *doesn't* do anything crazy. Understand?" I wink several times to emphasize that we're sharing a secret here.

"Why do you keep blinking?" she asks. "Is something stuck in your eye?"

Geez. Saving Mr. Dillon from humiliation is turning out to be harder than humiliating him in the first place.

The elevator doors open to a brightly lit corridor of concrete floors and gray cinder-block walls. We're in the bowels of the stadium. There are no Cardinals fans here. Unfortunately, there's no sign of Dee-Dub either.

I charge out and look from side to side. "Which way's the nest?" I ask Makayla.

"Just over there," she says, flicking her head to the right. "Why do you want to see it, again?"

I think fast. "I want to picture where your dad gets ready every day."

"That's just messed up," says Dynamo, shaking his head. "Why do you want to picture Mr. Dillon naked?"

"Who wants to see me naked?" demands Mr. Dillon, rounding the corner with Mom.

"No one!" we all shout.

"Good." He casts his eyes about. There's a panicked look on his face.

"Are you all right, Daddy?" Makayla asks.

"I've lost my keys, honey. I don't know how it happened."

Alyssa gives me a hard stare. Even Makayla narrows her eyes at me suspiciously. She's a smart kid—it won't be long before she demands to know more about Operation GMU.

"When did you last see them?" I ask.

"I don't know," says Mr. Dillon. "Maybe half an hour ago? I could borrow someone else's, but I need to find those keys!"

"These keys?" comes a voice from behind us. Dee-Dub walks right up to Mr. Dillon and hands over the key ring like it's no big deal. Like Mr. Dillon won't realize that Dee-Dub just *stole them.*

"Uh, thanks," says Mr. Dillon. "Where did you find them?"

Dee-Dub thinks about this for a suspiciously long time. "I think it was Section 160."

"So *that's* why you ran off," I say, smacking Dee-Dub lightly on the arm. "You wanted to return Mr. Dillon's keys, right?"

Dee-Dub looks completely lost. I'm not even sure he realizes I've just given him an alibi. But when I start to nod, he nods too, so at least it looks like he's agreeing.

Mr. Dillon *has* to know that Dee-Dub and I are hiding something. Alyssa seems to be holding her breath, like she's sure that Operation GMU is about to come crashing down and she's worried that everyone will think she's involved too.

Mr. Dillon steps toward Dee-Dub. He's going to call us out on our lie. I can see it in his face. I shrink back in my chair.

Instead, Mr. Dillon takes Dee-Dub's hand and pumps it up and down so hard, my friend looks like he's caught in a blender. "Thank you," he says. "Thank you *so* much."

Dee-Dub pulls his hand away. "You're welcome."

So far, so good. Except that I still don't know if Dee-Dub actually made it to Fredbird's nest. Did he finish Operation GMU?

But wait! He came from *behind* us, which must mean that he was still on his way *to* the nest. I can't believe our luck.

"Shouldn't you be going, Daddy?" says Makayla. "Fredbird's supposed to be out there already."

"Oh. Yes!" Mr. Dillon turns around and jogs toward the nest.

I have to admit: after all this excitement, I'm a little surprised that Mr. Dillon doesn't just come clean and admit that he's not really Fredbird. For a fake mascot, he's working really hard to keep up the illusion. No wonder Makayla still believes in him.

"I suppose we should head back to our seats," Mom says.

"Yes!" agrees Alyssa. "Oh, except I'm not in the same section as you."

"Hmm." Mom taps her lips with a finger. "It's quite a coincidence to find you at the game today, Alyssa. Any particular reason you're down here instead of in your seat?"

Alyssa turns bright red. "Just trying to make sure the boys behave themselves."

Mom laughs. "Good luck with that."

We file back into the elevator. Once we're all inside, Makayla continues to hold the door open.

"What are you doing?" I ask.

"Holding the elevator for my dad," she says. "This might be our only chance to talk to Fredbird."

Dee-Dub and Alyssa and I exchange anxious looks. A couple days ago, I was ready to unmask Fredbird. Now I want to protect Makayla from the truth. But if she hears Fredbird's voice, she'll *know* it isn't her father.

"Let's just see him later," I say.

"Good idea," says Alyssa.

Mom tsks. "Don't be silly. If Makayla wants to see her father, she should." Then she leans over and shakes Dynamo's hand. "I don't think we've met. I'm Noah's mom."

"Dynamo Duric," he replies.

Mom opens her eyes super wide. She's heard this name a lot over the past couple months. "Not *the* Dynamo?" she says, glancing at me.

"The one and only," says Dynamo. "I've got lots of imitators, but no one can replace the real thing."

Geez. Dynamo's ego is so big, I'm surprised he can fit into Busch Stadium. I'm about to say so too, when Fredbird leaps into the elevator. Makayla releases the doors, which close with a clank, and gives the bird a hug. In response, Fredbird reaches for his big feathery head, lifts upward, and—

I gasp. So does Dee-Dub. Because the face behind the mask is very familiar.

I stare at Mr. Dillon. Mr. Dillon smiles at me.

I think I'm about to pass out.

There are only two possible explanations for why Mr. Dillon is dressed as Fredbird.

(1) He just beat up the *real* mascot and stole his outfit.

(2) He *is* Fredbird.

As impossible as it seems, number two actually makes more sense.

Mr. Dillon claps a hand on my shoulder. "It's okay, Noah," he says. "Everyone gets tongue-tied when they finally meet Fredbird. But just remember: you can't let on that you know it's me, okay? I'm not supposed to be seen without the mask."

Before I can reply, a bell chimes and the doors open. Mr. Dillon slides the gigantic beaked mask over his head, leaps out of the elevator, and begins doing jumping jacks in the middle of the concourse.

I can't believe what I'm seeing. Mr. Dillon is a tank of a man, but put him in a Fredbird suit and he prances around like a ballerina.

Makayla cackles in delight. Mom chuckles. Even the mighty Dynamo gives a cheer.

Dee-Dub and I exchange glances. Did I say it was lucky we never went through with Operation GMU?

Scratch that—it's a freaking *miracle*.

FACE-OFF

While everyone else returns to our section, Alyssa and I stay behind on the concourse.

"So," she says, "I'll see you tomorrow morning at Berra Park. It'll be Logan Montgomery's last stand."

"It will be if you hit him in the leg again."

Alyssa wiggles her eyebrows. "That's my backup plan."

The concourse is emptying as Cardinals fans hurry to their seats in preparation for the start of the game. For several seconds, Alyssa watches them leave. Just as our silence is getting awkward, she crouches in front of me and takes my hands in hers. My palms are sweaty, but her fingers feel warm and smooth.

"This thing tonight," she says. "You know it was crazy, right?"

I bow my head. "I tried to call it off, but Dee-Dub—"

"Noah!" She squeezes my hands hard. I stop talking and look at her again. She has really pretty eyes. "I like you," she says. "A lot. I liked you even when I couldn't get you away from Logan and the rest of the morons you hung out with last year. But if you ever do something this stupid again, I will come after you with a baseball, and I will *not* be aiming for your glove. So promise me you'll grow a brain."

"I promise," I say, nodding quickly. I'll agree with anything Alyssa says because she's holding my hands, and she's beautiful and funny and cool, and I can't believe she really *likes* me, no matter how long we've known each other.

"Good," she says.

I think it's my turn to say that I *like* her too. Except I'll really be saying more than that, and my mouth has stopped working. I'm as nervous as I was when Dee-Dub handed over the keys.

Just say it, Noah.

Alyssa bites her lower lip, waiting. Then she stands, and I

know I've missed my chance. All the air seems to rush out of me at once.

No! I can do this. "I—I like you too," I stammer. "A lot."

Alyssa smiles. Her face brightens. Then she leans forward and kisses me lightly on the cheek. She even stays in place as I turn my head, so that for an instant our lips brush together. It's not exactly a Gabriella Masterson face suck, but our lips definitely touch. I feel like the world has just turned upside down.

"I'll see you tomorrow," she whispers. Then she bites her lip again, which is super cute, and strides away.

I watch her disappear along the concourse. None of the people walking past me seem to realize what just happened. How I just kissed Alyssa Choo. And to think: it never would've happened if Dee-Dub hadn't told Alyssa about Operation GMU, because then she wouldn't have come to stop us.

Sometimes, it helps to be an idiot.

Finally, I join the others in my section. They're all watching Fredbird. He's standing beside Dynamo's cheerleader sister and waving at the crowd, as restless as Logan after too many energy drinks.

Dee-Dub leans toward me and whispers, "I can't believe Mr. Dillon turned out to be Fredbird."

"You and me both," I whisper back.

"It totally ruins our plan."

"Shh!" I look around anxiously, but no one is listening. "It would've, yeah. Which is why we need to keep quiet. Just act normal, and no one'll ever suspect anything."

Dee-Dub thinks about this for several long seconds. "Someone's bound to find out eventually," he says.

"No way. Alyssa's the only other person who knows, and she's not going to tell anyone."

"What about the 43,975 people in the stadium?"

"What about them?"

"Well," he says, "don't you think they're going to notice when the itching powder starts to work?"

My stomach flips. My heartbeat races. I feel like I can't breathe and the world is spinning. "You're kidding," I croak.

Dee-Dub shakes his head.

"But . . . but . . . when we saw you, you were heading *toward* Fredbird's nest."

"Oh, that," he says. "Yes, well, I left the packet of itching powder in the room by mistake. I was going back to get it so there wouldn't be any evidence."

"Did you just say itching powder?" asks Dynamo, who has clearly been listening.

"Itching powder?" exclaims Makayla. "Who's got itching powder?"

Dee-Dub bites his thumbnail. "Oh, dear."

"What are you talking about?" demands Mom.

"Nothing," I say.

"Nothing," says Dee-Dub. "Except for Operation Face-Off."

"What's Operation Face-Off?" asks Mom.

"It's the new name for our plan," he explains. "Since Noah and I can't decide between Operation GMU and Operation MUD, I think we should go with Operation Face-Off." He turns to me. "You have to admit, it's far more descriptive."

He's right. It's a great name. If he'd come up with it a week ago, I would've told him so. Now I just want him to keep his mouth shut.

"That's lovely," says Mom, like it's not lovely at all. "So what exactly does Operation Face-Off involve?"

"It's complicated," I say quickly. "Way too complicated to explain right now."

"Not really," says Dee-Dub. "I put itching powder in Fredbird's mask."

"You did *what?*" Mom's eyes bug out. Her mouth twists into a really awkward position. She looks like a monster from a horror movie. "So help me, if Mr. Dillon—"

She shuts up as the national anthem begins. I can't stand up for it, but I place my hand over my heart. All around us, the stadium is silent and still.

Well, not completely still. Every few seconds, Fredbird twitches.

The young woman singing "The Star-Spangled Banner" has a voice as powerful as the stadium organ. When she's done, the crowd cheers loudly.

Fredbird doesn't cheer, though. Instead, he jerks his head like a mosquito has invaded his mask . . . or a thousand mosquitoes. Then, as everyone in the stadium claps their hands, our team's mascot claps his . . . head.

"Uh-oh," says Dee-Dub.

It's a pretty weird thing to watch a mascot smacking his noggin, and it doesn't seem to be helping either. Fredbird whacks himself again, harder this time. Dynamo's sister looks at her beaked costar like he's crazy.

"It's possible the itching powder is starting to work," says Dee-Dub.

I groan. "You think?"

Little by little, the stadium becomes quieter. The place is full, and everyone is tuned in to Fredbird's strange performance. The camera operators even project his image onto the giant screen across the park so that no one misses out on the craziness.

"He can't take the mask off," murmurs Makayla. "He just *can't.*"

A loud rock song starts blasting over the speakers. Fredbird throws himself to the turf and head butts the ground. Somehow, it's in perfect time with the music, and the crowd roars with laughter. Then, several people nearby start to mimic him, and others join in too, until our entire section is like a crowd of head bangers at a hard rock concert.

All around the stadium fans rise to their feet. They strum air guitars and sing along with the music.

On the baseball diamond, Fredbird launches himself backward and hits the ground headfirst. He flops wildly like a fish out of water, swings his arms at his head like a confused boxer, and slams his head back so fast it's like watching a whip crack. But through it all, Mr. Dillon refuses to take off the mask. It must be torture for him to keep it on, but some mascots aren't meant to be unmasked, I guess. Even ones who are going to wake up with some serious bruises tomorrow morning.

I ease my wheelchair backward, trying for a sly escape—in situations like this, it's important to rescue yourself first—but

Mom has her foot behind one of the wheels.

Makayla has a foot behind the other. "You're not going any-where," she says, eyeballing me.

Beside me, my genius best friend is chomping on his thumb knuckle like a starving baby with a chocolate-coated Binky.

"We need another plan, Dee-Dub," I whisper. "Seriously. How are we going to get out of this?"

He thinks for several seconds and announces, "Variables!"

"What?"

"That's the problem," he concludes. "Not enough variables."

Something tells me this is going to be a very long night.

MR. DILLON'S HIGHLIGHT REEL

The ride home isn't much fun. We ought to be celebrating the Cardinals' walk-off win in the bottom of the ninth, but no. Mom is fuming, Makayla's giving me the silent treatment, and Dee-Dub's probably trying to work out where it all went wrong.

"What were you thinking?" cries Mom for the third time.

I don't have a good answer, so I keep quiet. Unfortunately, Dee-Dub blunders in. "We believed that Mr. Dillon was being untruthful about his mascot identity," he explains.

In the rearview mirror, I see Mom frowning. "But *why?*" she asks him.

"Well, for one thing, Noah observed Fredbird at Makayla's school. Noah felt that the mascot's physical prowess was incompatible with Mr. Dillon's physique." After a moment, he adds, "Which is more like mine. We're both quite large, you know."

Mom sighs.

"For another thing," continues Dee-Dub, "we were under the mistaken impression that Mr. Dillon is a refuse consultant."

"How would you know that?" Mom asks.

"We hacked into the Cardinals' payroll accounts."

Mom almost runs us off the road.

"The refuse consultant thing is just a cover," Makayla pipes up. "It's like an alias so no one knows he's really Fredbird. He has to keep it secret. Otherwise, the paparazzi will be after him all the time."

I don't think the paparazzi are interested in a strange-looking bird with a bright yellow beak, but I don't say anything. Mom is driving really slowly, and I'm afraid she's about to dump Dee-Dub and me on the side of the road.

"What does GMU stand for?" Makayla asks.

"It's not called GMU anymore," replies Dee-Dub. "I changed it to Operation Face-Off."

"How can it be Operation Face-Off?" I ask. "Mr. Dillon never actually took off the mask."

Dee-Dub starts making strange sounds at the back of his throat.

"Fine!" I say. "Operation Face-Off, it is."

"Not if I have anything to say about it!" Mom snaps.

"We should've agreed on the name," says Dee-Dub, sulking. "Names are important."

"So are brains," adds Makayla. "You two should try getting some." Then she and Mom bust out laughing like this is the funniest thing in the world.

It could be worse. As long as Mom is laughing, she probably won't ditch us.

Forty minutes later, Mom, Makayla, and I are sitting in our living room, watching TV with the sound low.

Mom is bolt upright in her favorite armchair. "I only hope Odell can forgive us," she says, glaring at me.

"He will," chirps Makayla, eyes fixed on the TV. "He likes you, Mrs. Savino."

Mom turns on a smile. "Well, that's sweet of you to say. I guess he's got good taste, your father."

"He likes Noah too."

Mom's scowl returns. "Perhaps not such good taste, then."

There's a knock on the door. I shrink farther into my wheelchair as Mom goes to answer it.

The TV is on quietly, so I can just make out her voice and Mr. Dillon's. I can't hear what they're saying, though. Maybe that's a good thing—they're probably not sharing their favorite Noah stories right now.

Makayla isn't paying any attention to our parents because she's totally focused on the TV. The channel is ESPN, and the show is *SportsCenter*—specifically, the segment called "Top 10 Plays." At number four, there's an amazing catch by a Yankees outfielder; at three, an incredible goal by a European soccer player; at two, blurry footage of an elementary school kid who can already dunk a basketball.

"And at number one," crows the *SportsCenter* anchor, "the mascot for the St. Louis Cardinals redefines the meaning of crazy. Don't try this at home, kids!"

"Dad!" Makayla shrieks. "Come see!"

Mr. Dillon rushes into the living room at the very same moment that he appears on the TV in his Fredbird costume. I've already watched this routine live in Busch Stadium, but close up on the TV screen it's even freakier. The mascot contorts his chubby body like an Olympic gymnast. Who would've guessed that Mr. Dillon is as flexible as a Slinky?

Or he *was*. Right now, he's hunched over, and his face looks frozen in pain . . . or horror. At least, it could be pain or horror. It's hard to tell. Mom is in the process of slathering anti-itch cream across his cheeks, so he looks like he face-planted in a can of white paint.

On the TV, Fredbird throws himself headfirst onto the ground and head-butts the turf, arms and legs flailing behind him. Because this is *SportsCenter*, I figure they must have other stuff to show. But I guess not, because there goes Fredbird again, smacking his face, and tweaking his beak, and throwing his head backward and forward like an amped-up rock star. The show's anchors are laughing so hard, they're probably peeing their pants.

"Oh, my!" one of them says. "That is *serious* commitment from Fredbird, bravely going where no mascot has gone before."

"And where we hope no mascot will ever go again," adds the other.

"True that. I'm going to have nightmares about this for weeks. And to think, he kept this up the entire game!"

Swallowing hard, I look at Mr. Dillon. He doesn't seem to be moving much. I think he might need a night off after this . . . and a heavy dose of painkillers.

Makayla mutes the TV and turns to face me. So does Mom. So does Mr. Dillon. Even Flub raises one furry, wrinkled eyebrow. I don't like being the center of attention, especially not tonight. I wonder if this is what it feels like to face a firing squad.

"So," begins Mom, "what do you have to say for yourself, Noah?"

I open my mouth, catch a glimpse of Mr. Dillon's cream-smeared face, and close it again.

"I can't believe Noah got you on *SportsCenter*, Daddy," says Makayla. "I always knew you'd be famous one day, but I never thought you'd be number one on 'Top 10 Plays.'" She puffs out her cheeks. "Number one!"

All eyes shift to Mr. Dillon. Slowly, his pursed lips relax, and he begins to nod. "Number one is quite an achievement," he agrees.

"Quite an achievement?" exclaims Makayla, his personal cheerleader. "All over the country right now, people are talking about Fredbird. About *you*!"

His lips twist upward into a smile. "Number one," he murmurs. "Do you think I'm the first mascot in history to make it to the top?"

"Definitely! This'll probably never happen again in the entire history of sports."

"I bet you're right." Mr. Dillon raises his fist triumphantly. "Tonight, I scored a victory for the people behind the masks. This was for all the men and women in duck suits and bear costumes. For the ones dressed as sharp, pointy objects . . . and trees!"

Makayla frowns. "Trees?"

"Don't ask," says Mom.

"I showed everyone there's nothing a mascot can't do when inspiration strikes," bellows Mr. Dillon.

Mom shoots me a cold look. "Inspiration and *itching powder*," she reminds him.

"Whatever it takes. If I need itching powder to bring out my inner genius, so be it." Mr. Dillon looks at the tube of anti-itch cream drooping from Mom's fingertips and busts out laughing. "I'm just kidding. . . . Well, kind of. I really feel like I made a breakthrough today. I've been going through the same routine for years, but tonight, I rewrote the book on being a mascot. And now that I've done it once, I can do it again—without the powder next time."

He turns to me, smiling. I try to smile right back, but I still can't believe I might actually get away with this. Maybe that's what makes him suspicious.

"Tell me something, Noah," he says. "What exactly were you hoping to accomplish with the itching powder?"

I look at Mom and back to Mr. Dillon. It's time to come clean. "I wanted you to take off the mask."

"Well, yes. But *why?*"

"Because . . . because I thought it would be funny," I blurt out.

Okay, so maybe I don't want to come clean after all. And now Mom is glaring at me. I'm going to pay for this later.

"I see," says Mr. Dillon. He scratches his chin like he's thinking hard. Or maybe it's just because he's itchy. "And what about the keys to the nest? Did I drop them in your section, or did you take them?"

"Take" is code for "steal," and it's clear he already knows the answer. Mom shakes her head at me in disgust. I swallow hard.

"That was kind of my fault, Daddy," says Makayla

sheepishly. "Noah and Dee-Dub said they wanted to leave a surprise for you in the nest, so I swiped the keys. I didn't know the surprise was *itching powder*, but hey . . . it worked out great!"

Mom isn't buying this explanation at all, I can tell. But she doesn't want to accuse Makayla of lying when her own son is the one on trial. "Well, you're quite the team, aren't you?" There's an edge to her voice.

"Sure are." Makayla flashes a toothy grin. "Kind of like you and my dad. You're a good team too. Don't you think so, Noah?"

She just saved my butt, so I nod.

"You're not going to start sucking each other's faces, though, are you?"

"Makayla!" cries her father. "I told you: we're just friends."

"Friends," agrees Mom, blushing like crazy. "Really, Noah. You've got to stop teaching Makayla things like that. She's only nine."

"I'm only *nine*," Makayla parrots.

Then she winks.

It's like watching a younger version of Alyssa. So I do the sensible thing: I make a mental note to stay on Makayla's good side. If she's following in Alyssa's footsteps, I don't stand a chance of beating her.

But you know what? I don't think I'll have to. I get the feeling she's on my side.

I wink right back.

HOME RUNS

t's Saturday morning, ten o'clock, and Alyssa winds up
to pitch. The sun is bright against her cheek, and she's
squinting. Her hair is pulled back in a tight braid that means
business. She's playing to win.

The ball flies from her hand, curving in toward Logan's
body. He contorts his chest to avoid getting beaned. I catch
the ball in my mitt and throw it right back to her.

"Ball one!" shouts Mr. Riggieri.

"Seriously, Alyssa?" Logan sneers. "You're really going to
hit me again?"

She doesn't answer. Alyssa knows something that Logan

doesn't—the pitch wasn't her call. It was mine. Now that he's off-balance and scared of getting whacked, he'll be on the defensive. It's all part of my strategy.

There's a good crowd at Berra Park. Lots of the kids on the playground have half an eye on our game. So do their parents. It's a perfect day for watching baseball. Especially when the main players are a kid who looks big enough to be in high school, a really cute girl who's dressed like a bumblebee, and a catcher in a wheelchair.

I signal for the same pitch. Alyssa nods.

This time Logan falls over as he dodges the ball.

"Ball two!" shouts Mr. Riggieri.

"This is pathetic." Logan hauls himself off the ground. "Why don't you just walk me already?"

Alyssa returns a patient smile and sets about readying for the next pitch. It's a fastball. Dead center of the strike zone. The kind of pitch that Logan ought to smack all the way to Chicago. But he's convinced it's going to curve into him, so he hesitates. Watches it whip by and bury itself in my mitt.

"Stee-rike one!" exclaims Mr. Riggieri.

Logan's furious. Such an easy pitch and he totally missed it. He's probably vowing to hit the next one extra hard. Which is why he's way ahead of the ball when Alyssa gives him a pitch so slow it bounces a foot in front of him.

"Strike two!"

The game is no longer just between Alyssa and Logan. It's also between Logan and Logan. She's totally inside his head, and he's second-guessing everything. Things are going exactly the way we wanted them to.

Logan glances toward the playground like he's looking for inspiration there. I follow his eyes to a bench on the far side, where a powerful-looking man in dark glasses and a Cardinals baseball cap is watching us intently.

I recognize him instantly. It's Logan's dad, Coach Montgomery. But what's he doing here? And why are Justin and Carlos with him?

"Yo, Noah!" Alyssa is waving at me. "You still playing?"

"Huh? Oh, yeah. Right."

I signal for the original pitch: curling into his body. Alyssa nods. Winds up. Releases. But this time, the ball doesn't turn. Maybe the brief delay broke her rhythm or she lost control of the pitch, but it flies so straight it may as well be on a wire. Logan's ball-playing instincts kick in, and he swings. Makes perfect contact and sends the ball skyward. It flies like a bullet, heading toward a group of parents and kids in the far corner of the field.

I yell at the top of my lungs and point, but I can't tell if they're watching. If the ball hits someone . . .

A moment before impact, one guy reaches backward and casually bare-hands the catch.

"Uh . . . ," says Logan. "Did that guy just catch the ball bare-handed?"

"Yeah," I say. "You probably broke every bone in his hand."

I look up at Mr. Riggieri to see his reaction. He's standing beside me, a small smile playing on his lips, not because of the catch but because of the man who made it: his son, Marco. Phil is here too, and so is the rest of the Riggieri family—his daughters and grandkids. Mr. Riggieri looks like he doesn't know what to do.

Eager to get on with the game, Logan traipses across the dirt and takes the mound. Across the park, Marco throws the ball back to us. He's got a cannon for an arm, and the ball makes it all the way to the infield before bouncing once and hopping all the way to Logan's outstretched glove. For once, Logan is speechless. He doesn't often see throws like that in Little League.

Arriving at home plate, Dee-Dub picks up the bat and prepares for Logan's pitch.

"It's going to be a fastball," I whisper.

"Shhh," replies Dee-Dub. "I need to concentrate."

"I know," I say. "But I'm telling you: it's going to be a fastball. . . . Low and away."

"I don't know what that means."

"What? We went over this thirty minutes ago."

"Yes. But you never explained the terminology to me."

"Because you never asked."

Dee-Dub nods. "That was, admittedly, an oversight on my part."

Brows furrowed, Logan watches us from the pitcher's mound. All this talk between Dee-Dub and me has made him suspicious. And for what? Dee-Dub doesn't even know what I'm talking about.

So much for our pregame pep talk. All I wanted was for Dee-Dub to smack that fastball across the state line. He'd be a legend, and for once, it wouldn't be because of math. *Sheesh!*

I give Logan the signal for a fastball. From the way he hesitates, I think maybe he's on to us and is going to demand a different pitch. He doesn't, though.

I take a deep breath, relieved. Then I catch a glimpse of his grip on the ball, and I'm not so relieved anymore. His two top fingers aren't slightly apart the way they should be for a fastball. They're pressed together, the grip for his slider.

Dee-Dub doesn't stand a chance.

Logan winds up. I know what's coming, and instinctively, I position my glove down and to the right. Even though the ball looks like it's on a collision course with my mask, I trust Logan's pitch to curve away and hit my glove, just as it did hundreds of times last year when we played on the same team.

Poor Dee-Dub begins his swing, a giant lumbering swipe that will only shift air. Or will it? Because something crazy happens while the ball is in flight. With catlike reflexes, Dee-Dub bends his knees and extends his shoulder and suddenly the bat seems six inches longer. Long enough to reach all the way to the bottom corner of the strike zone. Long enough to make perfect contact with the ball.

With a deafening crack, the ball takes off. It careens toward the group still hanging out in the far corner of the park. As he did before, Marco Riggieri calmly steps up and catches it like it's no big deal.

Logan isn't looking at Marco, though. He's staring at Dee-Dub. "How did you hit that pitch?" he demands. "My slider's unhittable. Everyone says so."

Dee-Dub shrugs. "I recognized your grip. Your release and follow-through too."

"How do you know about different grips?" I ask.

"YouTube," he says.

Logan approaches the batter's box with thunderous steps. I really hope he's not about to start another fight with Dee-Dub. I guess Coach Montgomery is thinking the same thing, because he jogs over to us. Luckily, Logan seems to remember how well the last fight turned out and stops a few yards away. As his father draws alongside him, he scuffs the ground with his foot.

"Can you really do that?" Logan asks Dee-Dub. "See my grip and stuff."

"Apparently so," replies Dee-Dub, who seems as surprised as us to discover that it's true.

Logan looks at his dad. His dad looks at Logan. "Is this the kid who broke your nose, son?"

Logan sniffs and winces but doesn't answer.

"Yes, sir," says Dee-Dub helpfully. "That was me."

"Hmm." Coach Montgomery eyes Dee-Dub like a particularly dangerous species of bear. "What do you say we put that fighting spirit to better use?"

"You want me to train as a boxer?" asks Dee-Dub.

"Definitely not."

"A mixed-martial-arts fighter?"

"Huh?" Coach Montgomery looks exhausted already. "No.

I want you to try out for my Little League team."

"Oh." For maybe the first time, Dee-Dub, certifiable genius, looks completely stumped. "Well, I'll, uh . . . consider it," he says.

"'Cause I'm telling you, anyone who can hit Logan's slider is kind of useful."

"Looks like neither of us is unhittable, huh, Logan?" says Alyssa, joining us.

I wait for Logan's excuse: how he isn't feeling well or it was cheating to let Dee-Dub bat for us.

"I guess not," he says. "But that doesn't mean we're not both good."

Everyone falls silent. Has Logan's body been taken over by a peace-loving alien? Did Dee-Dub's punch to his schnoz knock some sense into him? One thing's for sure: I *never* thought I'd see the day that Logan said something nice about Alyssa.

"Is the world ending?" she asks.

"Must be," I say. "There's no other explanation."

"Are you feeling all right?" Dee-Dub asks him.

"What's the big deal?" complains Logan. He looks at his dad.

"Logan's right. You *are* good," Coach Montgomery tells

Alyssa. "And you'll be even better once you get some more control."

"And how am I going to do that?" she asks.

"With coaching, obviously. We coach all our players in Little League."

Alyssa gives him a funny look. "You want me to join the team too?"

"Why not?" says Coach. "You can pitch."

She returns a blank stare. "Uh . . . okay," she says.

"And you," says Logan, turning to me, "need to come back too."

Oh, geez. Here we go. I should've known Logan would want to get in one last dig at me.

"Don't tell me," I begin. "You want me to be the pinch runner."

Logan frowns. For a kid who's spent the past few weeks making terrible wheelchair jokes, he seems oddly uncomfortable with spinal injury sarcasm. Then again, no one else is laughing either. Maybe it's time for both of us to drop the lame attempts at humor.

Coach Montgomery straightens. "I was thinking more like an assistant coach," he says. "I just watched you and Alyssa work Logan for four pitches. And yeah, I might be biased, but I happen to think my son is quite talented. If you can get inside his head, you'll be performing Jedi mind tricks on weaker players."

"What do you say, Noah?" Logan asks.

Actually, I don't know what to say. I'm still not keen on spending quality time with Logan, but I want to be involved with the game again. And one thing is for sure: with Dee-Dub and Alyssa on the team, it'll be a lot more fun.

"Count me in," I say. "Assistant Coach Savino sounds pretty good."

"Maybe Mr. Riggieri could coach too," suggests Dee-Dub.

But Mr. Riggieri isn't with us anymore. He's all the way across the field, talking to the group of bystanders, especially the guy who caught our ball . . . twice.

"Don't tell me," Alyssa whispers. "*This* is the plan you were talking about in gym the other day." I nod, and she takes my hand. "Good. I like this one more than Operation GMU."

"Face-Off!" says Dee-Dub.

"Why didn't you call it Operation Mascot?" she says. "Sometimes simple is best."

Dee-Dub looks at me sideways. "Operation Mascot does make sense, Noah."

"Yeah," I agree. "Operation Mascot. I like that. Almost as good as Operation Reunite Riggieri."

We all turn to watch the miracle of Mr. Riggieri and his children coming back together. It's like whatever invisible force has been keeping them apart is breaking down before our eyes.

Dee-Dub rests his hand on my shoulder. "At least this plan worked perfectly," he says.

I can't help grinning. "Must've had the right number of variables."

Old Mr. Riggieri extends his hand to Phil and then changes his mind and steps forward to hug him. I don't realize I'm holding my breath until Phil and Marco hug him right back. I try to take a mental photograph of the image. Fathers and sons shouldn't be apart. Not as long as there's still the chance to be together.

"Anyone hungry?" Mom's voice comes from behind us. She's standing on the other side of the chain-link fence, taking everything in. Mr. Dillon and Makayla are with her.

"I am," says Dee-Dub.

"Seriously?" complains Logan. "It's only ten fifteen." He signals for Justin and Carlos to join us. Then he points at the

Riggieris, who are crossing the field. "If we can get everyone to play, we'll have enough people for a full game. That includes you, Mrs. Savino."

Looking uncertain, Mom steps around the fence to join us. Mr. Dillon and Makayla follow her.

"You owe me for this, Noah," Makayla says. But she's smiling.

Dee-Dub stands at home plate, loosely swinging the bat as Alyssa takes the mound. As I call pitches, Logan orders my mom to third base, and Makayla and Mr. Dillon to first and second. The Riggieri family spreads across the field. Most amazing of all, Logan tells his dad to umpire, and Coach Montgomery nods. I never thought I'd see the day that Coach took orders from his son.

The sun is warm, and the air is filled with the smell of pastries from nearby restaurants. The thirty or so kids on the playground are watching us, our very own cheering squad, as enthusiastic as mascots. It's fall, and the first leaves are turning, but this moment feels like a new beginning. As if anything is possible.

I know it's just my imagination, but as I look up at the clear blue sky, I feel like my dad is watching me. He would've loved a day like this. If he were here, he'd be lobbing me pitches that never come close to the target, and I'd be laughing as I stretched to either side to catch them. If Alyssa came along, he'd happily pick up a bat and let her pitch in his place. If Dee-Dub came along, he'd hand over the bat and stand on the sidelines watching and cheering. And maybe that's where he is now—on the sidelines, invisible but somehow present. Gone but always with me.

Time and effort, Noah. It's all just time and effort.

"I know, Dad," I murmur. "I get it now."

I look straight ahead and raise my glove, ready for the pitch.

Next play.

ACKNOWLEDGMENTS

It takes a village to raise a child. Luckily, Noah, Dee-Dub, Alyssa, and Makayla had a vast international community helping to bring their stories to life. In roughly chronological order:

My eternal gratitude to Ted Malawer, agent and friend, who read a few rather rough chapters of this book and told me in the clearest way that Noah's story needed to be written. To say you were all-in on this book from the get-go is an understatement, and I couldn't have done it without you.

Writing *Mascot* meant educating myself in the complex and traumatic world of severe spinal injuries. In an era when so much excellent information is available online, nothing was as eye-opening as my visit to the St. Louis Children's Hospital Neurorehabilitation Unit. Sincere thanks to Dr. Michael Noetzel, who set up my visit, and especially to Antonia Goelz, whom I shadowed for a morning. To see the bond between such determined kids and their unflaggingly enthusiastic care providers was inspiring. Any errors or misrepresentations are entirely mine.

Other St. Louisans were similarly generous with their time. In particular, I'd like to thank Mark Taylor, director of community relations for the St. Louis Cardinals, who answered a barrage of what must have seemed like seriously weird questions and gave me a personal tour of Busch Stadium, including behind-the-scenes access to Fredbird's nest. (Yes, I took photographs.)

During the writing process, I benefitted from the excellent feedback of my trusted beta readers: Jody Feldman, Brian Katcher, Clare John, and Dan, Deborah, and Jason Sorin. Thanks particularly to Audrey, Gavin, and Tamsin—you guys read this book more than anyone!

A big shout out to members of the fifth-grade book club at Kennard CJA, who took their roles as quality control experts very seriously: Indya N, Corinne F, Abby L, Grace F, Rachel T, Lola H, Andrew G, Lucy H, and Jalise B. And Brenda Kukay, club leader and school librarian extraordinaire.

In St. Louis and across Missouri I have enjoyed the friendship and support of countless librarians and teachers. I salute you all for advocating so passionately for books and readers. A special thanks to booksellers for getting my novels into readers' hands, particularly Sarah, Shane, and Cliff at Left Bank Books, who always brighten my day (and come up with the craziest ideas for book events).

Noah has found the happiest of homes at HarperCollins Children's Books, and I'm indebted to the whole team there: copy editors Jon Howard and Robin Roy; designers Aurora Parlagreco and Alison Donalty; publicist Ro Romanello; Meaghan Finnerty and Ann Dye in marketing; Patty Rosati, Molly Motch, Rebecca McGuire, and Stephanie Macy in school and library marketing; Sarah Homer, for her enthusiastic support and input; and Kate Jackson and Suzanne Murphy.

Finally, to my amazing editor, Tara Weikum, a million thanks. Your spot-on feedback has made Noah's story incalculably better, and your all-around good humor has made writing this book a total joy. Thank you for helping me to realize my vision, and for making me a better writer to boot!

KEEP READING

for a sneak peek at Antony John's next novel!

MOMMA'S WAKE-UP JUICE
ISN'T WORKING

t's Friday the thirteenth, and I don't think Momma will be getting up soon.

She was working late at the restaurant last night because Frankie, the boss's son, got sick. It's why she'll be in bed until ten minutes before the school bus comes to pick me up.

I don't like it when Momma works late. I always lock our door, so it's not like I'm scared. And the house is small and cozy—two bedrooms, kitchen, living room, and bathroom. But there's a space under our house, and when the wind blows hard, it makes this weird howling noise like a ticked-off dog. Last night, I called our neighbor Ms. Archambault so she could hear it over the phone. She's like my grandmother, only she's not family. Her house faces ours, so I can see her when she stands in her kitchen window and waves at me. Because Ms. Archambault owns our house, she promised to get her friend Ned, who's a handyman, to stop the howling noise. That sounded like a good idea to me. We don't need any ticked-off imaginary dogs living under us.

On the bright side, whenever Momma works late, I get to watch YouTube videos on her laptop. She thinks her laptop is password-protected, but my best friend, Kiana, told me to try typing in "pa$$word." When I told Kiana that it worked, she gave this long, deep nod, like she knew all along. Kiana wants to be a detective, like her dad. I think she's off to a good start.

Anyhow, today I let Momma sleep until precisely fifteen minutes before I need to leave the house. I eat my Cheerios, wash my bowl in the sink, and keep the water running so all the detergent bubbles disappear down the drain. I put my backpack by the door, wet my bobbed hair so it won't stick up in the back, and make sure my armpits don't smell. Momma says I have lax standards of personal hygiene. I don't know what that means, but I think it has something to do with needing to sniff my armpits more often. Finally, I pour a cup of *really* strong coffee and take it to her.

"I've got to go," I say.

She rolls toward me. "Toilet's over there," she mumbles.

I let out a long sigh. This isn't the first time Momma has used that joke.

"Are you coming?" I ask

She catches the smell of coffee but doesn't reach for the mug. "Oh, Lola, honey. How about you put yourself on the bus today? You can do that, right?"

I'm not sure how to answer. Sure, I can put myself on the school bus. The stop is only half a block away. But Momma has put me on the bus almost every day since I started kindergarten. Even when she was real sick a couple years ago, she hardly missed a day. Plus, she isn't looking at her coffee anymore. She calls it her "wake-up juice," but it's like she has forgotten the mug is there.

"Just this once," she murmurs, eyes closed. "I could really use a little extra sleep."

"Okay, Momma. I'll see you after your shift tonight, 'kay?"

"Same time, same place."

I lean forward and kiss her. She smiles. But she doesn't kiss me back. And she still won't open her eyes.

SHMORPEL BRAINS
AREN'T PRETTY

The worst thing about riding the school bus is Mallory Lewis. She's the second person who gets picked up, just two blocks after me. The bus company wanted her to wait at my stop, but Mallory's mom complained to the school that it wasn't safe. Now the bus picks Mallory up right outside her house. If you ask me, the only thing that would make my bus stop unsafe would be if I had to share it with Mallory.

"Hi, Mallory," I say as she clomps onto the bus.

She walks past me without a word. She's wearing really big headphones under her hoodie, but I don't think she would've answered even if she could hear me.

Mallory is three inches taller than any other kid in fifth grade. Which means she's three inches taller than any other kid in the *entire school*. It also means she's taller than half the teachers, and I think they're a little scared of her. That shows how smart teachers are.

How bad is Mallory? Let's just say she uses the kind of words that'd get you into *big* trouble at school. Whenever she does it, I cover Tiffany Gamble's ears because Tiffany's only five, which Momma says is an "impressionable age." I sure don't want Tiffany doing impressions of Mallory in front of her kindergarten teacher.

Tiffany gets on the bus after Mallory. She's small but looks kind of fierce, like a character in a movie who you just know is going to grow up to be a warrior princess. Or president. Her dad always waits with her. When the bus arrives, he gives her a bone-crushing hug and blows air kisses as she climbs aboard. Once she's in the seat beside me, he waves at me too and smiles big enough that I can see the gap between his two front teeth. I think Tiffany's lucky to have a dad who smiles like that.

Tiffany is a member of the Lola Harmon Book Club. To be precise, the only member. She's crazy about graphic novels, especially this series called Krunden and the Shmorpels, which her mom gets from the library. Every day, Tiffany hands me one of the books to read out loud. She has an incredible memory. If I read a book to her a few times, she almost memorizes it. Last week, she read one of them to her teacher, Ms. Kildare. Now Ms. Kildare thinks she's making "exceptional progress" at reading, which is impressive for a kid who doesn't seem to know the alphabet.

My friend Nick Merlo gets on the bus after Tiffany. He doesn't like riding the bus because Mallory keeps teasing him about his freckles, so I distract him by pretending not to know some of the words in Tiffany's book. That way, Nick can help out. It works real well, which is lucky because when Nick is annoyed, his face gets very hard and serious, like an igneous rock. "Igneous" is a word I learned in a science book. It means cooled lava, which is a pretty good description of Nick, if you ask me. Distract him with a book and he's all fire, and his smile gets crazy wide like a smiley-face emoji. But when he's annoyed. Well, like I say . . . IGNEOUS!

"Would you read to me today, Ms. Harmon?" Tiffany asks, rummaging around in her violet backpack. She has very good manners for a kindergartner.

"You know you can call me Lola, right?" I remind her. "I don't know if I count as a Ms. when I'm only in fifth grade."

"Are you married?"

"No. I'm in fifth grade," I say again, in case she missed it the first time.

She side-eyes Nick like she thinks I might not be telling the truth. Nick turns bright red. I don't know why. It's not like he's married either.

"Well, then," announces Tiffany. "If you're not married, you're a Ms. My mommy told me that."

Nick shrugs. Maybe his mom told him the same thing. My momma's never been married, so I guess she's a Ms. too. Seems weird for both of us to be called Ms. Harmon.

As the bus picks up more kids, Tiffany pulls a book from her bag and slaps it into my outstretched hand. It's the one we were reading yesterday—*Krunden: Shmorpel Killer*—so I open it up to where we left off. Tiffany leans into me, eyes glued to the page.

"'Krunden aimed his laser cannon at the shmorpel and fired,'" I read aloud.

The picture shows the pirate Krunden blasting an alien. It also shows the alien's head exploding, which gets me wondering if this book is really meant for kindergartners. I guess Nick's thinking the same thing, because his mouth is scrunched up real tight.

"Um, Tiffany?" I say. "Are you sure this book is meant for kids your age?"

Tiffany's eyes shift around. "Uh . . . yeah?"

"M'kay. Just checking."

I keep reading. The shmorpel's head takes a long time to completely explode. Two pages, to be precise. There aren't many words, but there are a whole lot of pictures. And all of them are kind of green.

Shmorpel brains aren't pretty.

Tiffany pinches the corner of the page and turns. "Ms. Harmon?"

"Yes, Tiffany?"

"You know how my daddy and your mommy used to date?"

"They went out for dinner *once*," I remind her. "I'm not sure that counts as dating."

"Well, anyway, you could've been my sister. I wish you were . . . my sister."

I lean into her. "But then we'd probably fight all the time," I say. "Like Nick and his sister."

Nick knows I'm kidding. He's really close to his sister, Katherine.

"I don't think so," says Tiffany. "I think we'd get along great. And if I had to share my daddy with anyone, it'd be you."

I've got to give it to Tiffany: She's a really sweet kid. Even if she's just sucking up to me.

"Where's *your* daddy, Lola?" she asks.

Nick's mouth gapes open. It's not a good look.

"I don't know," I tell her honestly. "Australia, I think."

"Where's Australia?"

"Other side of the world."

Her face creases up like she just got a whiff of a toot. "Why does he live *there*?"

"Because that's where he's from. He came here on vacation a long time ago. Then he stuck around longer than he should've. So they told him to leave and not come back."

Tiffany seems to be thinking hard. "Does that mean you've never seen him?"

I nod. "Yup."

"Oh." She stares at the dusty floor. "Do you miss him?"

"It's hard to miss someone you've never met," I say. But that's not completely true. I missed my daddy when I turned ten this past spring and realized he hadn't been around for any of my birthdays. It felt like a big deal, turning ten, and

I really thought he might call, even though he hasn't called in years. I just had this feeling he'd want me to know he still thinks about me.

I was wrong.

That was six months ago, but ever since, things keep reminding me of him. Like, I'll catch an Australian TV show and wonder if my daddy has the same accent as the actors in the show and if his hometown looks like theirs. Or I'll peek at Momma's old pictures of him and wonder how he might look today. I even think about how different things might be at home if he were around. Like every time the house makes a weird noise, or Momma can't give me a ride to Kiana's house, or she says she's tired even though she got more sleep than I did. Having an extra person in the house sure would be useful.

Tiffany wiggles the book to get my attention. The pages flutter like a butterfly's wings.

"Forgotten how to read, Lola?" Mallory sneers.

The other kids get quiet because they're scared of her. I wasn't thinking about her at all. She's sitting beside the emergency exit at the back of the bus with her sneakers propped up on the empty seat in front of her.

Nick's gone all igneous now, on account of Mallory being

mean to me. To distract him, I hold Tiffany's book up and point to a word like I don't recognize it. Nick furrows his brows and reads aloud: "Uh, 'lump,'" he says, sounding puzzled. "The word's 'lump.'"

Hmm. I should've pointed to a more difficult word. Now Nick might actually think that I don't know what "lump" means.

Mallory cracks up laughing. "Need help with any other big words, Lola? I could sound them out for you." She claps her hands like she's cheering for herself. "Hey, here's a new one: I-L-L-I-T-E-R-A-T-E."

I take a deep breath and remember what my neighbor Ms. Archambault said once, about how the only way to smother meanness is with kindness. True, she wasn't talking to me at the time. She was scolding her friend Ned, who never backs down from a fight and has the scars to prove it. But Ms. Archambault is very old and wise, and I've read enough novels to know that smart kids listen to old, wise women. Unless the old women live in houses made out of candy and try to cook kids in ovens, in which case smart kids should run away. *Obviously.*

The bus pulls up at our school. It always jolts when the driver brakes, like a horse bucking the rider, so I taught

Tiffany to shout "Whoa, Nelly!" But she's busy glaring at Mallory, so I'm the only one who says it today.

Mallory lumbers along the aisle and almost clips Tiffany with her bag. Tiffany slides her book into her backpack and slings the bag over her shoulder.

"You gotta stand up to her, Lola," she whispers fiercely. "Daddy says you can't let bullies win."

She's right. Maybe I'd have the courage to say so too if I had a daddy to back me up.